Praise for *Glory: The Gospel of Judas*

"A work of great stylistic and thematic importance . . . a stark and arduous book, the fruit of a continual re-reading of the 'Scriptures of the Eternal.'"
—Silvio Perrella, author of *Calvino*, praise
for the original Italian edition

"Berto's labor . . . is a mediation fixed to and developed on the joists of the Gospels, but where in the end, the upper hand belongs to the consciousness of our suffering and above all to the certainty of the futility and the impossibility of the word of Christ."
—Carlo Bo (1911–2001), Rector Emeritus of
the University of Urbino, praise for
the original Italian edition

"Giuseppe Berto's last novel is an original, relentless, and profound monologue, in which Judas Iscariot tells the story of Jesus and explains his own betrayal. Artfully translated by Gregory Conti, it folds past and present together and explores timeless themes of innocence, responsibility, sacrifice, and love."
—Francesca Parmeggiani, associate professor of Italian
and comparative literature at Fordham University

"Mastery of literary technique makes the reader sensorially present in first-century Palestine. One feels oneself to be Judas and relives his experience from the inside, shedding his prayers and tears over the dilemmas of loving, the enigma of evil, and the perplexity of being humanly free yet fulfilling a destined 'glory.' In this wrenchingly profound probing of the

T0283388

Glory

Titles in the **Other Voices of Italy** series:

Other Voices of Italy

Series Editors: Alessandro Vettori, Sandra Waters,
and Eilis Kierans

This series presents texts in a variety of genres originally
written in Italian. Much like the symbiotic relationship
between the wolf and the raven, its principal aim is to
introduce new or past authors—who have until now been
marginalized—to an English-speaking readership. This
series also highlights contemporary transnational authors,
as well as writers who have never been translated or who
are in need of a fresh/contemporary translation. The series
further aims to increase the appreciation of translation as an
art form that enhances the importance of cultural diversity.

Berto's *La Gloria* was published shortly after the author's
death in 1978 and never translated into English, despite
dealing with a well-known narrative and its main theme
having great appeal for large audiences. While retelling the
Passion of Christ, *Glory: The Gospel of Judas, A Novel* takes
the point of view of Judas, the traitor who was accused but
never allowed to defend his actions. By mixing betrayal and
responsibility with prophecy and predestination, this fresh
account problematizes the interaction between defector and
victim to show the blurry lines of Judas's actions. If his
betrayal was announced prophetically, how can Judas be held
responsible for it? This is the question the novel asks before
coming to the conclusion that, thanks to his betrayal, Judas
was in fact a crucial instrument of salvation. Berto's revision of
the biblical text bears at once the mark of a humble defense
of the voiceless protagonist but also the prideful remake of
the divine word from a thoroughly human angle. Betrayal
becomes a figure of speech for the transmission of events and
the inevitable stumbling block between reality and fiction.

Glory

~

The Gospel of Judas, A Novel

GIUSEPPE BERTO

Translated by Gregory Conti

Foreword by Alessandro Vettori

Rutgers University Press

New Brunswick, Camden, and Newark, New Jersey
London and Oxford

Rutgers University Press is a department of Rutgers, The State University of New Jersey, one of the leading public research universities in the nation. By publishing worldwide, it furthers the University's mission of dedication to excellence in teaching, scholarship, research, and clinical care.

Library of Congress Cataloging-in-Publication Data

Names: Berto, Giuseppe, author. | Conti, Gregory, 1952– translator. | Vettori, Alessandro, writer of foreword.
Title: Glory : the gospel of Judas, a novel / Giuseppe Berto ; translated by Gregory Conti ; foreword by Alessandro Vettori.
Other titles: Gloria. English
Description: New Brunswick : Rutgers University Press, 2024. | Series: Other voices of Italy | "Translation of La Gloria. RCS Libri, 1978."— Title page verso. | Includes bibliographical references and index.
Identifiers: LCCN 2023035434 | ISBN 9781978839571 (paperback) | ISBN 9781978839588 (hardcover) | ISBN 9781978839595 (epub) | ISBN 9781978839601 (pdf)
Subjects: LCSH: Jesus Christ—Fiction. | Judas Iscariot—Fiction. | LCGFT: Christian fiction. | Novels.
Classification: LCC PQ4807.E815 G5713 2024 | DDC 853/.914—dc23/eng/20230808
LC record available at https://lccn.loc.gov/2023035434

A British Cataloging-in-Publication record for this book is available from the British Library.

Translation copyright © 2024 by Gregory Conti
Copyright © Giuseppe Berto Estate
Published by arrangement with The Italian Literary Agency
Translation of *La Gloria*. RCS Libri, 1978.

♾ The paper used in this publication meets the requirements of the American National Standard for Information Sciences—Permanence of Paper for Printed Library Materials, ANSI Z39.48–1992.

rutgersuniversitypress.org

Wilt thou also disannul my judgment?
Wilt thou condemn me, that thou may be righteous?
—Job, 40:8

Contents

Foreword

The Betrayal of Judas

What happens when authors attempt to rewrite the Bible? They can do so for devotional purposes as an exercise to better comprehend its meaning and offer a more satisfactory interpretation of it; or they may be deemed blasphemous for appropriating a sacred text and bending it to their needs without possessing the legitimate preparation and authority to do so. When their choice of texts falls on the Passion of Christ or the portrayal of Judas Iscariot, and their revision involves reconsidering crucial facts about Christian salvation, they are bound to be considered sacrilegious and their undertaking totally desecrating. Giuseppe Berto's *Glory: The Gospel of Judas, A Novel* is neither of those two things. It is a lucid— at times uncomfortably logical and brutally impassioned— revisiting of one of the most (if not the most) crucial episodes of the New Testament, its causes, and its consequences. Berto's constant search for clear answers to insoluble existential dilemmas takes him to biblical texts as possible guides to his questions, but his approach remains literary, at best philosophical, never theological or dogmatic.

An uncompromising and unwavering secular writer, Berto is nevertheless fascinated by religion and the answers it may afford a restless and inquisitive mind like his. Because of his familiarity with Christianity (he was raised in the Veneto region in the first decades of the twentieth century when faith was a determining factor in the culture of his people), he uses the Bible and the Christian tradition as a gold mine from which he extracts themes and crucial experiential issues related to life and death, love and hate, loyalty and betrayal, and familial relations, among others. The biblical text remains a constant reference for his writing, and starting from his first novels, he uses it to grasp the deeper meaning and purpose of life. Many titles of his works are inspired by the Bible, *The Works of God* (*Le opere di Dio*), *The Sky Is Red* (*Il cielo è rosso*), *Man and His Death* (*L'uomo e la sua morte*), *The Passion according to Ourselves* (*La Passione secondo noi stessi*), *Glory* (*La gloria*), and even when the title does not reveal it, the Bible provides a hypertext the author consults and often makes reference to, in order to contradict and modify it thanks to his creative renditions of it.

Always in search of answers to complex questions regarding death, guilt, and especially evil and betrayal, Berto remains existential and if not atheistic at least agnostic, rejecting the self-assured answers religion proposes. This explains his attraction to the biblical book of Qoheleth (also known as Ecclesiastes), which expresses doubt that one can ever know God's plan for humanity and also distrusts divine justice. Qoheleth questions the meaning of life and death and wonders if good and evil obtain remuneration on earth. The absence of definitive answers being its main feature, the book feeds on the paradoxes of death giving life, eternity meeting transcendence, and betrayal serving salvation. This is the biblical text that most appeals to skeptics like Berto and Judas.

The quest for a father figure permeates Berto's novels and becomes a leitmotiv of his entire oeuvre, while also making it more attuned to the Judeo-Christian tradition that identifies God with the father. The exploration of biblical texts becomes a personal mission to clarify the author's relationship to his own father and his role in shaping his worldview and his writing vocation. This fascination with the father figure finds multiple incarnations in numerous novels, to culminate in *Il male oscuro* (*Incubus*, 1964), the story of the protagonist's fraught relationship with his father and his attempts to make sense of it through psychoanalysis. The father-son relationship, which bears unmistakable autobiographical traits, constitutes a perfect fit in the picture of Christianity as the religion of God the Father in his relationship with his Son Jesus.

The rewriting of the Passion from the perspective of Judas in *La gloria* is provocative because it gives voice to the person who has been accused of betraying Jesus and causing his death; history has, therefore, silenced him and relegated him to eternal damnation next to Satan. In his own version of the facts, Berto's Judas explains in the first person and from beyond time how not his own determination through free will but rather predestination guided his actions; his most unsettling deed consists of interrogating divine justice for delegating the responsibility to a single person for the redemption of others. What is Judas's real responsibility if prophets had announced his betrayal from time immemorial? Did biblical announcements make him simply a passive instrument, or did he have agency and freedom of action? Why was he held responsible for betrayal if he had been predestined to it? If Jesus's death was essential for redemption, the terms of the equation can, in fact, be reversed and Judas can be considered the source of salvation itself, his betrayal the fundamental instrument to bring it about.

Eliminating all canonical and theological interpretations, Berto sees Judas as the real protagonist of salvation; he logically argues that without Judas's betrayal there would not have been the essential passage of the crucifixion leading to redemption. Judas's betrayal comes as an "act of love," as obedience to a role that was decreed for him since the creation of the world. The insoluble paradox between predestination and free will makes him the most interesting literary character of the Gospel narrative, and Berto's fictional rendition casts aside Judas's responsibility to emphasize instead the painful condition of being relegated to this role by destiny.

Betrayal is at the center of *La gloria* as the event that determined Christian redemption and changed the course of history, but the story also questions predestination and providential intervention in human endeavors. In his first-person monologue, Judas highlights the unfairness of being destined to his role from the beginning of time and being accused and condemned for his responsibility in turning Jesus over to be crucified. The paradox turns into an existential aporia that has no other effect than casting him into the role of a loathsome accuser, the worst enemy of humanity, and the damned soul by antonomasia. Berto appropriates the biblical story and transforms it into an intricate human event pointing out all the incongruities of the canonical version, while chipping away at its monolithic structure and opening it up to further discussion. The fictional rendition of the Passion problematizes betrayal as a theme, but also casts it as deceiving the original text in rhetorical terms as a figure of speech of rewriting. The present translation into English from the original Italian offers additional energy and substance to the accumulation of versions and increases the sense of a gradual detachment from the facts as they really happened and how they were first reported in the

Gospels. Betrayal, whether intentional or involuntary, factual or rhetorical, acquires more tortuous connotations to do with the reconstruction of "reality" and the literary value of its reconstruction.

The best trope that describes Berto's reworking of the Passion is parody, intended not as mocking, disrespectful elaboration of the referenced text but as a neutral remake of it, which in fact elevates and praises its value by trying to imitate and transform it while highlighting its most intimate essence. The term "parody" is to be understood, therefore, as a retracing of the original text from a different angle and a different perspective, so that the rhetorical exercise exemplifies what is implied in the etymology of "parody," which literally means "accompanying song" or "countermelody." The change in perspective allows for an increased understanding of the original. While this rewriting has many positive connotations, it can also be perceived as a deconstruction of the original, which inevitably ends up losing the mystical/ mythical aura of untouchability. The new version, therefore, also reconsiders and assesses the sacredness of this specific text in the Christian tradition. Betrayal is the theme of the novel, but it is also the figure of speech that identifies it. Parodying the Passion betrays the monolithically orthodox and officially accepted interpretation of it.

Judas's Messiah in *La gloria* is not the Redeemer, God's son who was sent to save humanity, the initiator of a spiritual renewal who came to free people from sin; he is rather a social reformer, a political activist, whose main mission is to rebel against the Roman invaders and restore peace to his people—and that is why Jesus of Nazareth so disappoints Judas, who feels that his expectations for a political reformer and social activist have been betrayed. Judas views Jesus's actions as betrayal, and not the other way around. In fact, he considers his own deception a service to humanity instead of treachery. He obeyed the command, fulfilled the prophecies that predicted his treason, and obtained redemption for humanity in the process.

La gloria is Berto's last novel, in fact a posthumous book that came to light a few weeks after his death on November 1, 1978. There was no better way to conclude this author's literary trajectory than with a narrative that recasts, adapts, and personalizes the Passion of Christ by putting Judas at the center of it as first-person narrator and protagonist. Judas's death by suicide parallels Jesus's crucifixion, which Berto attributes to Jesus's passive acceptance, if not downright intentionality and desire for death. Judas's first-person narrative, emanating in an atemporal, postmortem dimension, from beyond historical reality, elevates the novel to a metaphysical sphere and gives it the power of an otherworldly pronouncement. The death of Berto between the completion of the manuscript and its publication casts Judas's narrative about Jesus's crucifixion into a cycle of death and afterlife that seals the novel as fulfilment of the writer's career and, within the fictional frame of *La gloria*, an accomplishment of Judas's mission as reassessed in his own terms. The big questions the novel asks—but never tries to give an answer to—are about the relationship between individual predestination and free will and the role of intentionality in the larger scheme of history that is preordained or guided by divine providence. The inconclusive verdict speaks clearly of an inextricable tie between them that is impossible to disentangle, even in the metanarrative of the novel's rewriting, which technically "betrays" the preordained referenced text with a provocative, diverging version.

The concept of glory for Berto becomes increasingly more ethereal and symbolic, from simply being a synonym for his literary "success" to secular interpretation of the theological word as manifestation and acknowledgment of his merits. In Berto's usage the word is closer to the Greek *doxa*, meaning "reputation," "fame," and "glory," but also "opinion," and since the last book deals with a new, provocative perspective on the Passion, the word "glory-doxa" as translating "opinion" seems the most adequate, at least in rhetorical terms. The fact that the author died shortly after completing this novel about suffering and death—and an attempt to find a plausible explanation to it—gives a renewed meaning to the word *gloria* and to the novel bearing this title.

Alessandro Vettori
Rutgers University

Translator's Note

Although I'm sure it is only coincidental, it certainly feels right that I should be writing this on the morning of Holy Thursday, the day of that Last Supper in Jerusalem that Leonardo and Veronese and other Renaissance painters would later make into an icon of Western civilization. In chapters 96 to 99 of *Glory*, Giuseppe Berto memorializes the dinner scene as the key moment in his novel, when Jesus, in fulfilment of the scriptures, designates Judas Iscariot to be His betrayer. "Nevertheless, the word of the scripture must be carried out. One who eats the bread with me has raised his heel against me." Thus, Jesus, and Berto, express the paradox that lies at the heart of the Gospel of Judas: he who would be forever condemned as the betrayer of Christ was prophesied and destined to be the betrayer by God himself: "He who welcomes him whom I have sent [Judas] welcomes me and he who welcomes me welcomes him who sent me." Judas, as Carlo Bo would write in a 1979 foreword to *Glory*, was "the figure necessary to the theater of the ultimate tragedy."

Berto's decision to tell the Gospel story from the point of view of Judas was certainly part of what compelled me to translate *Glory*. Taking on the task allowed me to revisit my memories of all the references to the betrayer that I had heard in sixteen years of Catholic education, from elementary school through university. As I worked on the translation, however, I was increasingly intrigued by what I came to consider a more interesting and current question, namely, what, if anything, is the value of Berto's testamentary novel for non-Christian or nonreligious readers? While I cannot claim that my answer to this question is impartial or disinterested, I nevertheless feel that Berto's retelling of the Gospel story is of interest even to nonbelievers because it raises and examines a mystery that all of us, the faithless as well as the faithful, are faced with at times in our lives: the mystery that good sometimes comes from evil and, conversely, that evil is often a consequence of good. As he tries somehow to come to terms with his own destiny, Berto's Judas finds inspiration, and perhaps some consolation, in the words of the great poet of the book of Ecclesiastes, Qoheleth: "'But there is no man on earth capable of doing good without doing evil.' Perhaps the Eternal had also ordained the contrary, that there was no capacity to do evil without doing good." Berto's *Glory* does not in any sense resolve this mystery, nor does it attempt to, but it does help us to recognize it as an essential element of human experience.

Gregory Conti
Perugia, April 6, 2023

Author's Note

All the quotations from Qoheleth or Ecclesiastes are in the translation of Guido Ceronetti (Einaudi). The quotations from the Book of Psalms and the Book of Job are partially by Guido Ceronetti (Einaudi) and (Adelphi) respectively. For the Gospels I used the translations appearing in the Oscar edition published by Mondadori. [Trans.: All relevant citations were translated directly from Berto's Italian text after consultation of the authorized King James Version.]

Glory

1

Never, at no time in our arduous history, not during our enslavement in Egypt or Babylonia, our harrowing journey toward the Promised Land, or Saul's mortal war against the Philistines, never had we been so lost and divided, never our souls so fallen in the dust and the looming shadow of death.

Why are you sleeping, O Lord? Why do you turn your face away from us, fail to make your voice heard? How are we at fault?

The King of the Jews took his authority from Rome. From the towers of the Antonia Fortress, the soldiers of Caesar dominated the Temple. The sound of their trumpets—outrage and warning—struck Mount Zion. We were the fable of the infidels, the shaken heads of peoples, revilement for our enemies.

Nevertheless, there was little deep sorrow. The High Priest and the Sanhedrin agreed with the idolatrous Procurator on what was to be done. To obtain some advantage, to protect our people, they said, we mustn't give the occupier the occasion to wreak havoc. Where is your might? Where are the feats you accomplished in the days of old? Scribes and Pharisees debated the essence of the law with vacuity and cunning; whether the letter should prevail over the spirit or vice-versa, or some prudent blend of the two.

Caravans traveled through the East, and from the East toward Jaffa and Caesarea—the ports of Rome—and the merchants went about their business, not respecting even the sacred places. The young maidens sang God is our refuge and our strength, succor always available in every misfortune, but it was their voices that sang, not their hearts. The people lived from day to day, in a picturesque pandemonium, practicing the various trades with which the poor customarily survive, including thievery, certainly, and prostitution, and worse.

The zealots, on the other hand, our best and restless youth, said that the silence of the Eternal—which had lasted now for four hundred years—was about to come to an end. The extermination of those who oppressed and scorned us was near. They advocated resistance and rebellion, secretly kept their spirits afire and their daggers sharpened, but it all seemed very unlikely. Every now and again the Romans arrested someone—a common criminal—and put him on the cross, without anyone really knowing how they managed to nab him. Fearing informants, people whispered, and insidious suspicion made its nest everywhere. Betrayal, a word destined for a much higher end.

The Book, as should be obvious, was discussed everywhere with erudition; the promises made by our Eternal God to his chosen and blessed people, the flattery and the threats, the by now imminent coming of someone—Elias, a Prophet, the Messiah—who would untie all our knots and soothe all our torments. But the impression was that it was all empty talk, that the faith was more than anything else a rhetorical exercise or a tired habit. The frail expectancy of the kingdom was mixed with the fascination of idols—the tenacious longing for the golden calf, the new seduction of the multiple gods that comforted the occupiers. All things considered, it was also possible to fear that Israel was a miniscule and labile nation, dwarfed by the boundless empire of the Romans, destined to become a province, with no civilization of its own; with no God of its own. Those who had been to Rome spoke with amazement and apprehension of massive crowds and legions, spectacles and rites, grandeur and splendors, compared to which what we were in terms of number and greatness seemed, in the silence of the Eternal, something ridiculous, which it was legitimate for those who were all around us, and over us, to deride and scorn.

A difficult faith, ours, and many children of Israel were, in the present, distant from their God, with hardly any fidelity to the pact.

This in Jerusalem, the Holy.

2

Elsewhere, in Judea and Galilee, throughout the brief land where our Eternal God was pleased to place his people in order to reside with them, the grandeur of Rome found nothing to measure itself against, the soldiers of Caesar did not push themselves into regions so deprived of significance, nor could the sounds of their trumpets be heard. There, the people living outside of history but inside the pain of living, could not distract themselves from believing, were in more fervid expectation of Him whom the Book said would come. Praying together was their way of asking and waiting, boundless humility and still more boundless superbity were part of their relationship with the Eternal. Yet they did not go so far as to hope for, and perhaps not even to think about—when it came right down to it, it really wasn't any business of theirs—One who with whoops of war would put all the other nations of the Earth, starting with Rome, obviously, under the dominion of Israel.

They were simple folk, with no limit to their simplicity. They didn't have sufficient cognizance of the thirst for power of kings—even if they were anointed by the Lord—so their faith tended instead toward heavenly paths. They imagined that He whom the Book had been promising for centuries—and who now would finally come because it was time he came—would return his chosen and blessed people, who had tirelessly persisted in awaiting him, to the condition that was theirs in the beginning. As was written in the Book, in the beginning our Eternal God had planted a garden in Eden so that his people could live there without the sweat of their brow or the pains of childbirth or the anguish of death, and to this garden, where there was no pain of living—or pain of death—his people were to return as soon as the Eternal One had sent One who, breaking the interminable and inexplicable chain of expiations, and taking upon himself the responsibility for the first knowledge and for all the other innumerable sins that the people so estranged from God had committed, would bring about redemption: the reunification of creation with its creator.

Now, on the margins of the rocky deserts, where nothing but thistle bloomed with its purple flower, on the mountains of Samaria, where in summer the herds went to pasture, on the sweet hills of Galilee and on the shores of Lake Tiberias, where the trees grew tall and the fields produced wheat and flax in abundance and the waters gave up fish in abundance, in the many insignificant villages scattered about the promised and given land, there lived a people who felt the presence of Our Eternal God not only at birth and death, at prayer and meditation, but also in any other activity or thought, in feeding themselves and going to the market, in plowing and harvesting, in waking up and going to bed, in lighting the fire and listening to the wind, and this meant being Israel, the chosen and blessed people.

3

I, Judas Iscariot, born in Jerusalem of a merchant father, raised in the shadow of the Temple, educated in the law and scripture, observant of the norms and precepts, bound to the zealots by conspiracy and having fled from the holy city to avoid the cross, was traveling the lands of Israel, anxious that the Eternal Adonai should manifest himself by showing me a sign of his mightiness, or of his vanity. I was young, and impatient.

Until when, O Lord? Buckle your sword to your side, and in your magnificence lead us on the attack in your chariot, for the cause of freedom, truth, and justice.

But the soldiers of Rome were standing atop your holy hill, and they imposed tributes, and as for the rest, traveling around your lands one inevitably happened to come across those born blind, those possessed by the devil, shouting volleys of oaths; and far too often the beating of sticks with which the lepers warned people to stay away. In the face of all this, I was tempted to ask myself where the Eternal was, and if there really was an Eternal or rather an infinite void, an infinite nothingness as sung by Qoheleth, son of David, King of Jerusalem, and he had also sung in his brief impassioned song: the only good thing man has under the sun is to eat, drink, and be merry. This was written in the Book.

So then, why couldn't I, Judas, manage to be splendid and profligate? What profit did I get from all my suffering, from all the torturing of my heart? What did it bring me, all my labor under the sun?

I interrogated myself, interrogating the Eternal, and the Eternal remaining silent, I had to concede that I should find a sort of glory in all of my suffering, a glory that was perhaps perverse. Proud self-deprivations, audacious prayers, nurtured boundless ambitions. I was strong and brave, the equal of a king; I mustn't lose myself. Was this not also said in the Book with the words of kings? Do not give your vigor to women, nor your customs to those who lose their kings.

Virtue was power, therefore I hated sin.

4

But sin was everywhere, not only in Jerusalem. It was found
obscurely mixed with prayer and hope, charity, and love, and
it was quite possible that the roots of this confusion of
sentiments were remote, the knowledge of good and evil
contained in a single fruit having been the first endless
transgression.

In effect, there were sinners among the Levites and
among the faithful: among the potters and the masons; the
shepherds and fishermen, and surely there were adulteresses
among the women who washed clothes in the stream, or
drew water from the well; among those who spun and weaved,
who thrashed wheat on the doorstep or kneaded bread, and
the prominent people who did their praying at the head of the
line were undoubtedly sinners too; the bosses who didn't
pay a just wage, the judges who neglected the law. There was
sin in those who lent money at usurious rates, or collected
taxes, or who brought food to their mouths without thank-
ing the Eternal, and there was also sin in me, because of
my impatience, of my continual doubting and questioning,
but it was the vastness itself of sinning that spawned hope,
so much darkness necessarily called not for mercy but for
redemption, the Eternal could not persist in his inordinate
silence, otherwise the chosen and blessed people would be

lost, dissolved in the immense empire of Rome. Where was the presence of the Eternal?

When it is time I will act quickly, he had promised.

5

What was, in the will of the Highest, the right time?

The hour is near, and this is it, the people repeated, and many asserted that the Awaited, the Messiah, the Lord's Anointed, was already to be found among us; that he was already making his voice heard to those who would understand it—but the will could also derive from necessity—and in truth, never had the lands of Israel, from Dan to Beersheba, been crossed by so many messengers and prophets and pilgrims of God, who preached amidst fog and enigmas, speaking with words that they proclaimed to come from the Eternal, and sometimes working wonders, with a power that they swore came from the Eternal.

They went from village to village, outside the houses and inside the synagogues they announced the good news, they called on God as their witness and some of them even managed to perform a miracle, that is, when things went well, by dint of invocations and exhortations a deaf-mute would begin to talk, a person possessed would calm down. Then the people would celebrate him, bring him gifts, organize banquets.

Almost always, even before the banquet had ended, the deaf-mute went mute again and the person possessed relapsed into his obscure malady, and then it was understood that it was not with the force of God that he had worked, but with the aid of Beelzebub, the enemy of God, and this only added to the confusion and disorientation of Israel, so that the poor imposter had to rush to grab all his things and clear out of town to avoid being stoned, and, if he was a total charlatan, he would head over to another village to restart the enterprise of earning himself a banquet, but he might also head out into the desert, where there were rocks and wind and solitude, where it was easier to interrogate the Eternal, and easier to die.

Impenetrability, as always. Was it sleight of hand, trickery, fraud? Or crude will to power with the involvement of demons? Or religion, as false as you want, but originated by illusions and not in complicity with the Evil One? Moreover, if our God was one and all, how could he leave someone or something outside of himself? And again: why the suffering, the ignorance, the doubt? And the impatience?

6

With impatience I went searching, on the tracks of so many improbable prophets, for some glimmer of revelation; subtle signs. Try as they might, the improbables could not seduce me; I knew how to distinguish an arm capable of raising a sword against Rome, eyes in which there was some manifestation of spirit, a voice that somehow resonated with the breath of Adonai. Yet even they, especially the most melancholy and foreordained, in some way expressed the anxiety of the chosen and blessed people, the disappointment over the long silence of the Eternal, the urgency that, if the Coming One were to come, he not come too late.

The land, promised and given, was now under the dominion of the infidels, and the pain of living in that land was no less than elsewhere, nor less grueling than in the past. Were we perhaps to expect even greater misfortune?

Hence, among that people closest to the Lord by prayer and honesty of living, there were rumors that the Awaited was already among us, but hidden, and hard to find. The difficulty, we thought, was the work of God, so that everyone would apply themselves with dedication and diligence—certainly not impatience—to the discovery of the Anointed. Perhaps he would not be revealed unless we did something more than we were then doing to make him reveal himself.

This must have been the meaning of the exhortation of the just: be ready, vigilant, the hour is near, and everyone was in the throes of anxiety, that is, practically speaking, inclined to fall into the grossest of errors.

7

Nevertheless, among the many and contrasting rumors that were circulating, there was one that seemed more serious and substantial, and it concerned a man who, his soul alien to women and to comfort, fasted and refrained from drinking wine. Nor did he even perform, as far as was known, great prodigies, but he witnessed to God and baptized with the waters of the Jordan. To baptize meant to restore purity to body and soul, to give the benefit of grace, and the authority to do this could not but come from the Eternal. It was not certain that he himself was not the Anointed, but, all things considered, his following was not so numerous as to lead one to think that he could accomplish the feats that everyone thought were to be expected of the Awaited.

I had made the acquaintance of someone who had been baptized by him—his name was John: the Baptist, they called him—and those whom he baptized were not all that different from anybody else, they seemed to be afflicted by the same difficulties as always in terms of poverty or the pain of living, only their spirits seemed to have been touched, more persuaded that the revelation of the Messiah was near, and with it the end of all suffering, and they believed it simply because they had been told so by him, the Baptist, in whom for some inexplicable reason one could not but believe.

Always demanding, this faith of ours.

How is it that this preparation for the advent—or the advent itself according to those who thought him to be the Anointed—came about with so little splendor and power, one baptism at a time, or small groups of people who then returned to their homes to do the things they had always done, with unaltered fatigue? This was not how one could imagine the day as ardent as a furnace, the redemption of a people so in need of redemption. And then, what to think of the domination of Rome? These baptized believers gave no sign that they cared about it, often didn't even know of it, perhaps in dependence on a new activism of their spirits.

There was something that needed to be understood in all of this. I set off in the direction of the Jordan. He was said to be on the left bank, in the land of the tetrarch Herod.

Indeed, He was there.

8

What the people said corresponded to the truth: he didn't have a numerous following, twenty or at most thirty, all men. They were together in a group on the shore of the river chanting prayers, and every now and again he baptized someone, invoking the Most High, pronouncing words that I couldn't quite make out.

Neither did he have an arm to raise a sword against Rome, nor did his voice, from the little that one could hear of it, sound like it possessed the breath of the Eternal. But his gaze, yes, entranced and intense at the same time. It had something that came from farther away than him and continued on far beyond us. It expressed a universal appeal for help, not for himself who asked, he being only an agent, but as part of a higher endeavor in which the role assigned to him had by now been entirely carried out, or nearly so, since, as far as he was concerned, he was already wearing his death, not the death from loneliness or desperation that the dubious prophets went looking for in the deserts of stone, but a death of martyrdom, of blood.

I saw it on him when I got up close: a red mark around his neck. And I shuddered, for him and for myself, because I too had a mark around my neck; not so red as his, however, not so imminent. At times, mine faded almost to the point of disappearing, perhaps signifying a destiny which might even change.

For his, there would be no changes: what he did was full of faith, or at least of inspiration; reflected at the same time ineluctability and conviction.

9

I was still there when a delegation of priests and Pharisees arrived from Jerusalem, sent by the Sanhedrin to investigate, that is, to determine if by chance this man's following, and his words and actions, were such as to worry the institutions of power, that is to say, in the first place, the Roman procurator, Pontius Pilate.

The arrival of these deputies was a bit ridiculous. They themselves felt out of place, so conscious were they of the disparity between the meagerness of the facts before them and their own authority and culture. Nevertheless, since they were there, they did their investigation and, having approached the supposed prophet who was the cause and object of their long trek from Jerusalem to the Jordan, they asked him, somewhere between commiseration and insolence, "Who are you?"

He, however, who could read their minds as he could read the bottom of a clear stream, answered fully: "I am not the Anointed."

A few of those fools started to laugh, but others, even more foolish, continued the interrogation: then, who was he? Elias? Or a prophet? What authority did he have to baptize people? How was it that he was authorized to bear witness and preach?

He replied that he was only the voice of one who shouted in the desert to give warning that, the advent of the Awaited being near, the people needed to prepare themselves, that is, to straighten the way with penitence and purity of living, and he added that he committed no sin baptizing with water, but, he further added—and prophetically turned to the onlookers the gaze that bore a sign of the Eternal—in your midst there is one whom you do not know.

That's precisely what he said, with a voice suddenly vibrant, as he turned his gaze to us—to me—with its sign of the Eternal. And I, with that flash of his gaze upon me—a flash for me alone, he did not intend to neglect me—felt a trembling of my soul, desire and repulsion, trepidation and exultation, unfathomable premonition. I waited for something unspeakable to be revealed to me, perhaps a mysterious designation, but his entranced gaze, rife with portent, had already moved away, leaving me in a profound, fearful temptation. And if the Anointed, Coming and perhaps Come, were still not fully realized in his power and sanctity, but must instead take shape gradually, becoming? If, so to speak, he already was, but still had to acquire consciousness of his own being through signs and suggestions, shudders and commotions, and the concourse of others—emissaries of the Eternal—as was happening to me?

Chasms are the pronouncements of Adonai, impenetrable his actions.

Overcome with fever I rushed away from there, headed back up the valley toward the east, on the arid hills strewn with briar patches that could also have caught fire. Was this the mightiness of God or that of Beelzebub, the enemy of God, that had inflamed me under the gaze of the Baptist? Election or infernal pride?

All night long, on my knees, I interrogated the Eternal.

10

All night, O my Eternal God, my impatience suffocated but not my fever, I interrogated you: prostrate, dismayed, gasping. Spread your grace over those who love you, and over the pure, your goodness.

I am not impure, O Lord, and I love you.

You are the salvation of believers, and I believe. You are the One, the Name.

Above me, in the expanse of the heavens, the stars you created on the fourth day preside over the night, boundless immensity: and it is you. And inside of me, my soul, other boundless immensity, given that you wanted me in your image and likeness. And if I am so conflicted inside my soul, this too is a likeness because in you, Adonai, there are predilections and repugnancies, abandonments and recoveries, patience and disgruntlement, your inscrutableness is light and mystery, bewilderment and destination, but always sanctity, while my spirit is convolution and abyss, and human fretfulness, but who, if not you, has filled my heart with such immeasurable anguish? From whom, if not from you, came the authority of the Baptist's gaze?

Then answer me, my Eternal God: am I the Messiah, the promised King, the Anointed?

If you give me not a sign, how can I be certain of it? Eternal One of the hosts, all of my desire lies before you, my soul is bold and faithful, my arm is able to raise the sword of David, and I can offer you my death on a battlefield of victory.

But tell me: am I the Awaited?

Leave me not, Lord, be not distant from me, my God, help me now, my Lord, my salvation. Yours is the power. Your voice penetrates the desert, fills up the valleys, makes the waters tremble, shakes Mount Zion from its foundations.

Or is your voice the silence?

11

Stars rose over the rim of the mountains, climbed above me as others rose behind them, and then it was morning; the light from the east erased the endless night during which I had so long been seduced by the why of my being, of my existence.

The Eternal had given no response to my questions, but his voice possibly being silence, I would have to attain clarity in other ways. I would go down to the river.

The early morning awaited with purity the hours that were to come, the sunlight bathed the declining hills with happiness, the valley floor was ever so slightly veiled by a luminous mist that would soon dissolve. Everything sang out glory to the Eternal in the land given to us, the chosen and blessed people, among whom he would be manifested, as promised. And it was time, the expectation of the Awaited, in painful uncertainty, having become too great.

The night spent on my knees interrogating the silence had not exhausted my spirit or mitigated my fever. Now, approaching the river, I would ask the Baptist, in whose eyes was the sign of the Eternal, with all possible humility and without impatience: "Tell me, am I the Messiah, the Awaited, the Anointed of the Lord?

He was not an immensity of silence, and I would welcome any response of his, ready to take responsibility and command, but also to make my way toward the desert of loneliness and rocks.

12

Many people were walking down to the river on that clear morning. I found myself walking not far from a figure surrounded by a small group of followers—ten or at most twelve—who was making his way absorbed in his thoughts, or simply intent on not tripping over the rocks and the rugged spots on the wide path. When they spoke to him, those who were gathered around him called him Rabbi, and he responded in a very soft voice, if he responded at all. He was handsome—he the most beautiful of the sons of men—and tall in stature, but slight; neither was his arm such as to preoccupy the members of the investigative committee, if by chance they were still in the vicinity. But they had gone, it seemed.

I mixed in with his followers—country people with unrefined speech—and together we headed toward the Baptist.

He was standing on the riverbank, he too surrounded by no more than a dozen people, ready to take up his daily chore again, and he didn't look as though he were expecting anything out of the ordinary. But then, noticing that we were coming his way, he became agitated, and in an excited, high-pitched voice, much different from what he had been able to produce the day before, he started to shout:

"Behold the Lamb of God who takes away the sins of the world!"

It was an exalted way of speaking, which surely needed interpretation—what was lamb of God supposed to mean? Why not shepherd, for example? And then: take away sin?— but the vain wait for answers had dug deep in my soul an anxiety that those words, as obscure as they were, would have been able to placate, had they only been directed to me.

But it was immediately clear—the sudden immobility and celestial presence all around him—that they had been said for the one whose followers called him Rabbi.

I should have rejoiced, given that I had been going from land to land in search of a Rabbi, and instead I felt bitter, not so much out of rivalry or disappointment, but because I had been put on notice that in my vainglory I had been influenced by the spirit of the Evil One.

Meanwhile the Baptist was explaining to his little group of followers that he who had just arrived was truly the one of whom he had said that after him there would come one who was greater than him because he was prior to him. Ever more confused his manner of speaking, nor did his voice, as hard as he tried, have the breath of the Eternal.

Both the Rabbi and the Baptist were about thirty years old—my age—and nobody who saw them could have said who came before or after, assuming he was talking about years and months and not of hidden things. In any event, the Rabbi, not visibly affected by the enthusiastic welcome, went down to the river and immersed himself up to his waist, and the Baptist, his hands cupped, gathered up some water and poured it over his head, pronouncing on high the usual incomprehensible invocations, when out of the blue he started shouting like a crazy man: "I have seen the spirit descend from heaven in the form of a dove; testimony that this man is the son of God!"

The affirmation was such as to provoke exultation, glory, panic, bewilderment, and terror, or at any rate excitement. Instead, it didn't have much effect on those present, perhaps because that was precisely what most of them were expecting, or perhaps also, because of the abundance of the self-proclaimed sons of God who in those times were wandering about the promised and given land, they had become inured to such announcements.

In any event I, who deep down was still brooding over my disenchantment, knew that no dove had come down out of the sky, and I was struck by the painful suspicion—more bitter than my bitterness—that there was an understanding between the two of them.

But the evidence was against this. The Baptist, who had an aversion to women, who fasted and did not drink wine, who had as a garment—his only one presumably—a colorless camel hair blanket with a leather string around the waist, who had that ugly mark around his neck of which he must have been aware, who was not, frankly, very handsome to look at or possessed of any appreciable strength, he, in other words, couldn't have had any earthly interests such to justify the hypothesis that he was a bamboozler.

There was no choice but to come up with some other solution.

I went over close enough so that I could look right into the face of that Rabbi, and I saw that his gaze—that never came to rest on me—had the power to subjugate. I found myself thinking, being overcome with emotion and confusion, that I would die for him—which later came to pass—if he asked me to, to fight against Rome, or for any other reason. He had that power, which certainly came to him from on high, and therefore it was very likely that he was capable of making someone shout that doves were coming down out of the sky even when, actually, no one had seen even the shadow of a dove.

13

Actually, history—the new Book, says that—sometime later, the Baptist having been imprisoned—the mark around his neck became redder and redder every day, such that it was not granted to cultivate great hopes or fears regarding his fate— and reaching him even in jail news of the wondrous works of that Rabbi who, perhaps on an impulse of complaisance, he himself had solemnly proclaimed to be the son of God, had sent some of his loyal followers to him to ask: "Are you he who is to come, or are we to wait for someone else?"

This was, on the part of the Baptist, an evident manifestation of perplexity, and yet also of optimism, if he really thought, in his circumstances, that he still had time to wait.

On that occasion, the Rabbi had responded to his questioners in no uncertain terms that the extraordinary prodigies he performed were authentic, and he added: "Blessed are they who do not waver in their faith by reason of my person."

A few days later, the austere and wavering Baptist had his head chopped off, at the capricious behest of the king, it seems, or of the queen. But he who had sent back such a harsh response had some suffering of his own to look forward to.

His name was Jesus, and he was from Nazareth in Galilee.

14

You derived from Nazareth and that, according to the way of thinking back then, was not exactly good fortune. It was said, in fact, that that remote village, though in all respects similar to other remote villages in the land of Israel, had the prerogative of not producing memorable events or personages. Can anything good really come from Nazareth? Nevertheless, You, whom your followers called Rabbi, were surely not without resources, and perhaps not even a ne'er-do-well.

You wore a garment that could have been worn, for example, by a tradesman, and you wore no jewelry or ornaments of any kind, but one could see on You—it was part of You, of Your beauty—a regal quality that not all kings possess: a majesty, of which it is not certain whether it is earthly or divine.

What sort of advantage was to be derived from this, in teleological terms, is not, even today, all that clear, given that the many misadventures that were then lying in wait for us were not, it seems, conducive to universal resolution. But back then, in that moment, in the wake of the prodigy of the dove which, as dubious as it was, was believed by many, the lineaments and the expression of Your countenance, the gaze, the gestures, the voice—I overheard you saying to your followers a meaningless phrase, which in fact was not reported by Your biographers: "Rest yourselves, we will leave here this afternoon"—transmitted the impression of a spiritual measure that drew on something much higher than human nature, which was nevertheless humbly proper to You.

In sum, it may well have been that in You the spirit had become flesh, as was later said, and at the same time this is something that, to some extent, happens to everybody. But the portion that fell to You was, if it can be put this way, disproportionate, and therefore disproportionate was the force that emanated from You.

Maybe Rome wasn't to be fought only with swords, and anyway sometimes our forebears had had victory not from their arms, but from Your right hand and from Your arm, O Adonai our God.

15

Off to the side with the Baptist, he too ate roots and drank water, giving thanks to the Eternal. Then, when the sun started going down behind the rugged hills that separated us from Jerusalem, he called his followers together and headed south, where the hills were even more rugged and desolate. Nevertheless, they were lands that the Eternal had given to us.

I followed them, at a distance, deep in thought: neither lighthearted nor worried. I didn't feel I was running any risks—his followers were poor souls, certainly not violent—and for the rest, I had already followed more than one unlikely prophet. He was a few steps ahead of his little group, walking together with his thoughts.

He might not have been the Anointed, the one responsible for the final glory, but the Baptist—leaving aside the dove—had spoken of him with conviction, openly declaring him greater than himself. So, even assuming that he was not the Anointed, maybe he still had something to do with the Awaited, the one that was to come to save our people from our enemies, and to placate our disquietude, mine included.

It was to my advantage that I follow him while, with his poor little entourage, the night drawing near, he was walking in a direction that pointed to the desert. It could even be that, after the adventure and the satisfaction of the baptism, he too was heading off to the rocks, to question and die. This Rabbi was the best of the lot that I had happened into up to then, and I was following him from reason, or perhaps fascination, not from faith.

But faith, as would be said later, is given, there is little or nothing we can do about it.

16

Paul later wrote that, one must walk behind You from faith and not from vision. This means perhaps that the enchantment that one feels on encountering You must go down deep and become some other thing, while remaining, in the last analysis, enchantment. To faith in You, to believing in the hoped-for substance, I came, if indeed I came, very late. In effect, when You wanted me to want to: You know all there is to know about enchantments.

However, that night as I was following You while You were going toward the desert with Your tiny following, it was not that I was totally enchanted. I kept asking myself if You were really the Anointed whom I was searching for, or if You had only built up within Yourself that splendid and tremendous conviction of which I had not been capable.

Besides, we didn't even know what, reasonably, we should expect from one awaited so anxiously, and with so much confusion of ideas. Surely, he would have to be a king—and You had all the majesty of a king—and he would have to lead us, we the chosen and blessed people, in the name of and with the force of the Eternal, but toward what exactly he should lead us we were not all agreed.

The best youth of Jerusalem, for example, had no doubts: toward liberation from the Romans and to the subjugation of the others, different from us.

Ordinary people, on the other hand, dismayed by the pain of living and still more by the necessity of death, imagined a return to Eden, where, it was hoped, there would be none of the lamented circumstances.

Finally, the intellectuals, who seemed to be in possession of more reliable information, talked about the acquisition of vaguely defined goods, which had to do, in any case, with an eternity of eternity. Even conceding to the intellectuals the right to be obscure, it is clear that there exists only one thing that is so interminable.

Many centuries later, an American Jew, he too with his fair share of torment, asked himself, and the Eternal: what is the philosophy of this generation? He found, I hope with the help of the Eternal, this singular response: "Not that God is dead, that period ended long ago. Perhaps it can be stated this way: Death is God."

You are, therefore, splendidly modern, Jesus of Nazareth, and I fear that You will continue to be so, until mankind will have found the way to reach the end of time, or, as You were more wont to say, glory. But—we cannot cease to ask ourselves—why was it not reached then? What was lacking for the final achievement—the death of God—the connection between the particular and the universal, or something else? Was there impatience or, worse, haste?

Son, enjoy life. Qoheleth admonished us: follow where your heart goes and the gaze of your eyes.

Again, Paul thought, it seems, that You had an earthly life tending, from the very beginning, to condense itself in death. It's true: that was where Your heart was heading, and the gaze of Your eyes, but You were not the only one, that day by the river, to have that kind of tension. Both the Baptist and myself bore our own signs, and furthermore it is known that death is not inexorable for everyone; for some it is temptation, or even hope.

My heart and the gaze of my eyes had no uncertainties that day; they were going to You, and if then I followed you, instead of staying with the Baptist, it was because You were going toward a death much higher than that which can be attained by way of the caprice of a king, or of a queen. It is not that in such a way I was to enjoy my youth, or the part of my youth that remained, but there was no other choice.

17

Or was there, aside from Your enchantment, another choice?

The Book doesn't help us very much to understand—
that-which-is has already been, what-will-be has already
been—nor do You help us. Mark refers an answer of yours:
"But to sit on my right hand or on my left is not for me to
give; but it shall be given to them for whom it is prepared."
I would like to know: did You respond that way because
James and John were importuning You with vain questions
or, really, beyond Your and our power, was something destined for someone among us? And if something to someone
why not everything to everyone? Even my death? Even yours?

We died more or less at the same hour. You crucified on
Golgotha, I not far away, hanging myself, from a fig tree—
if it is really true that it was a fig; it's one of the least suited
trees for hanging oneself—exemplifying a sin—known as
final impenitence—to which it seems mercy must be denied.
Ignominious conclusion. But Your death on the cross, which
in the intentions of those who wanted You dead was not to
be any less ignominious, became, little by little, apotheosis.
Yet, at the time, everything came about with extraordinary
simplicity, at least if we go by the version of John, the one of
us that You loved more than the others, who, nevertheless,
in that supreme moment, was worried more about himself

than You, and perhaps that too must be taken into account, in reflecting on the failed achievement.

John recounts then, that, crucified between two thieves and after urging Your mother who was standing at the foot of the cross to take him as her son, You were thirsty, and the Roman soldiers, who for some reason had to follow the words of David, gave You vinegar to drink, and after drinking the vinegar You said: "It is done!" Then, Your head bowed, You gave up Your spirit.

Whatever was accomplished in that moment You had no way of explaining, and as for John, it is better not to look too deeply into what he wrote, otherwise one might come away with the impression that what You had to accomplish You accomplished by urging Your mother to take him as her son. Above Your head there was a sign saying You were king, and the deaths of kings are always rife with sordid stories of succession. And I, who was expecting the final accomplishment, understood that there was nothing for me to do but hang myself.

Thus, mankind is still here, toiling away between the pain of living and the anguish of death, but You are called Lamb of God, Redeemer, Savior, while I bear a name that signifies betrayal. In our story, where the Manichaeans of all times have found comfort, You are the light and I am the darkness. We have comforted innumerable cruelties and injustices. It is not possible that the darkness is only darkness—nor perhaps the light only light—but because it seems that mankind cannot do without cruelties and injustices, I continue to be the darkness: he who betrayed, who delivered him up to his enemies, about whom few words are wasted.

About You, almost too much has been written, too many hypotheses formulated, so that everyone has seen You—and sees You—in his own way, sustaining himself with You for good and evil, peace and war, rectitude and deviousness, poverty and wealth. They have used You—and they use You—to constitute fraternities and tyrannies, to celebrate and to persecute, to succor and to afflict. How many of Your followers have forgotten that, for You, operating on this earth with justice—and love—has never been an end, but a way toward taking one's place, when the feat will have been accomplished, in the kingdom of heaven?

18

Your father—but he wasn't in point of fact Your father—was named Joseph and he worked as a carpenter in Nazareth. You, in accordance with certain prophecies, were supposed to have had the blood of the kings of Israel, and so two evangelists did everything they could to construct for Joseph some astounding genealogies. One went back to Abraham, the other all the way up to Adonai by way of Adam, with illustrious personages in between, some of whom were rather wicked—the kings of the chosen and blessed people are incredibly full of atrocities and lasciviousness, in addition to sanctity. In this way, the carpenter could claim Davidic descent, but You, of his blood, had no share.

Here, in fact, is how Your birth came about. Mary, Your mother, was engaged to Joseph, and before they went to live together, she found herself pregnant by work of the holy spirit. Joseph, knowing nothing of the holy spirit, wanted to have her tried but, since he had no taste for scandal, he made plans to break the engagement privately.

In the meantime, however, a messenger from the Lord appeared to him in a dream, reminding him that there was a prophecy concerning the matter—the virgin will conceive and will bring to the light a son and he shall be called Emmanuel. Joseph obeyed and took the woman with him, and when You were born he called You Jesus instead of Emmanuel. This seems to have been the only sign of contestation in the whole story. Apart from that, one can only imagine the resignation, and perhaps also the sadness, of this good man on whom was imposed such an extraordinary adventure.

In a village like Nazareth—nothing good ever came from there—a story of fecundation by work of the holy spirit could be, if known, accepted religiously, but also, potentially, interpreted with scorn. They were not very inclined to credulity, nor to charity—as will be seen—the people of Nazareth. Not a very comfortable situation for a carpenter, especially one with Davidic descent, and it is known that the frustrations of fathers, even of putative fathers, have repercussions for their children: they can easily give rise to inferiority complexes.

On the other hand, the virgin mother had no alternative other than to insist, with pride, on the truth of the version of the conception through the intercession of the holy spirit. She showed herself exultant because the Most High had turned his gaze on her, his humble servant, and surely thousands of times, giving You milk, changing Your clothes, rocking You to sleep, she will have said and repeated over and over that You were the living son of God. This could have given rise to a superiority complex, which then, acting from the subconscious, gives one the force of conviction of which another is incapable.

Then, partially because of a census issue and partly because of prophecy, You were born not in Nazareth, in Galilee, but in Bethlehem, in Judea, during the reign of King Herod the Great. A little while later, there arrived in Jerusalem from the East three magi. They brought with them precious gifts to offer to the king of the Jews who was supposed to have already been born—they had learned it from the stars—and they went around asking where they might find this new king about whom, by the way, nobody knew anything. King Herod, superstitious and insecure, became very worried and, after consulting his own astrologers, he decided to suppress all the male babies, under two years of age, in Bethlehem and its surroundings.

This happened: the king's soldiers—here too a prophecy was involved—tore the babies out of the arms of their mothers and stabbed them and quartered them with their swords. There was crying and great lamentation. Rachel cried for her children and would not be consoled.

You, however, were spared. Warned in a dream by the messenger of the Lord, Joseph escaped with Mary, carrying You to safety. Who knows how many times this extraordinary adventure—the flight into Egypt—was retold to You when You were a child; proof of a special vigilance over You on the part of the Eternal. But You, as You were growing up, perhaps You will have begun to ask Yourself if, to demonstrate to You his solicitude, it was really necessary that the Eternal should bring about a slaughter of innocents. This could have given rise to a guilt complex, the thought that someone would have to pay for such a mysterious injustice.

19

Many centuries later, a French writer, meditating on the terrible agony that You chose for Yourself—chose, he says, and to think that he wasn't even a believer—had the idea that the real reason for that choice was that You knew that You were not completely innocent with regard to the butchered innocents. "I am sure he could not forget them. And as for the sadness that can be felt in his every act, wasn't it the incurable melancholy of a man who heard night after night the voice of Rachel weeping for her children and refusing all comfort? The lamentation would rend the night. Rachel would call her children who had been killed for him and he was still alive!"

Very well said, probably, but You, that death of Yours into which from the very beginning Your life had been condensing itself, You never thought of it as a reaching of individual peace, and even less as payment for an ethical debt. Things were much more tangled than Camus imagined, and the sense of guilt nestled in Your subconscious did not lead You to pay for a slaughter, but to make it so that slaughters would never happen again. Your dimension was always universal.

Anyway, there is no doubt that the singular events surrounding Your birth and Your adventurous survival immediately marked with blood had weight in the shaping of the structure of Your psyche. You found Yourself divided between the flattery of being the Anointed, come from the eternity of the spirit, and the presentiment of having to pay a price that was bound up with death. This was Your drama right up to the end, when Your agony was called passion.

Nevertheless, as long as You were a child in Nazareth, with a father who resignedly worked his wood, and a house-wife mother who told You, as though it were a fable, the sublime tale of the fatal annunciation of the angel, the desire to be the son of God knew no obstacles.

In effect, You reached the certainty of being him surprisingly early, as recounted by Luke.

20

Luke recounts that when You reached the age of twelve Your parents decided to take You to Jerusalem for the feast of Passover. It was the custom, back then, to go to Jerusalem for that feast; to spend a few less monotonous days, to buy some things that were not available in the villages, and above all to pray in the Temple that Solomon son of David had built to conserve the Ark that housed the Name, the Divine Presence. The Temple was the center of the faith and culture of the people of Israel, and it seems that children—at least the most promising ones—having reached a certain age, were presented to a committee of priests of the Temple that would assess their religious and civil education.

The journey to the capital from distant regions such as Galilee took several days. To travel more safely—the route passed through lands infested with thieves—the pilgrims traveled in small groups of family and neighbors, and along the way they joined up with other groups as their numbers grew larger and larger. During the journey, the travelers made new acquaintances, exchanged information, and formed new friendships. Then, having celebrated the feast, the groups retraced their steps on the journey home. Usually, they moved out at the first light of dawn, in the midst of a great confusion: the quadrupeds had to be looked after—given to drink and fed before setting off—loads redistributed, supplies and provisions checked, all accompanied by shouting, calling back and forth, and some occasional cursing. The children, excited and playful, were usually given the task of providing the drinking water, which they got from springs using gourds, or little canteens made from leather or canvas.

When—just before sunrise—the caravan that the people of Nazareth were part of set off toward the north, You were not with them. Your parents, however, were sure that You were nearby, and when, later on, during the day's journey, they didn't see You, they were not worried: the children got bored walking with the adults, they preferred staying together to laugh, play, and make plans for future games and adventures. But in the evening, when the caravan stopped for the night and You didn't show up, they started to worry. They went from fire to fire looking for You, inquiring of relatives and acquaintances, and they ceaselessly prayed to the Lord, and called out to You, all night, even after the voices and the songs of the pilgrims had quieted.

The next morning, while the others were setting off for Galilee, they turned back full of apprehension and even remorse, because they felt they hadn't been sufficiently diligent in looking after You, although, at twelve years old, intelligent and thoughtful boy that You were, it was legitimate to think that You wouldn't get lost in a city that, big though it might seem, was no more than half hour's walk from end to end. They looked for You in all the places where You had been together: streets and crossings; squares and markets; inns and taverns. Finally, after three days, they also looked for You in the Temple, and that's where they found You, sitting among the elders, posing to them, You a twelve-year-old boy, the most profound questions.

It was a scene that inspired wonder, and even pride, but they, the carpenter from Nazareth and his wife, were still in the throes of the anguish of those four days during which they had been more and more afraid that they had lost You, maybe forever. So, beyond the joy of having finally found You, Your mother's question was a mixture of pain and admonishment: "My son, why have you done this to us? Your father and I have been searching for you and we have been in pain."

To this observation—humble, all things considered, but after all one of the principal virtues of the virgin mother was her humility—You, still a boy, responded with arrogance. Were You euphoric over the success You were having with the elders? Were You ashamed, there in that setting, of their provincial behavior? The fact remains that You responded: "But why were you searching for me? Didn't you know that I must be about my father's business?"

They, to their good fortune it can be said, did not catch the sense of Your words, didn't understand that You had already freed Yourself from Your melancholy and frustrated father, from Your exalted and possessive mother, that by now You were ready for Your earthly and heavenly mission, on behalf of another, and more satisfying, father. But, at twelve years old, what could You do? You returned with them to Nazareth, and the Book says that from then on You obeyed them docilely.

21

Because of this docile obedience, many of Your most zealous followers can now say that You were a worker, a member of the proletariat. That doesn't ring true. Even if You hammered nails and sawed boards, being a carpenter was not Your condition. You studied, prayed, meditated, dreamed, pretty much as I did at the same time.

For one night—just one interminable night—I was tempted, with desperate hope, to believe myself the Anointed, the Coming One, without taking comfort either inside or outside of myself. The fault of my little faith, or of the circumstance that I had a father who was not only putative, and a mother who was aware of having conceived me quite regularly.

You, slowly but surely, sitting down to table with Your parents and helping the carpenter to saw and plane, grew in knowledge, stature, and grace before God and men.

When You felt You were ready, having turned Your back without weeping on Mary and Joseph, Your brothers and sisters and the hovels of Nazareth, You set off to find the Baptist.

And I was there.

22

They stopped a little after sunset, near a well with some young trees growing around it, bent by the wind. The landscape had rapidly turned to desert. When the sun went down the air immediately turned cold. When I went down to the well, they hardly looked at me, nobody said a word. Some of them were rummaging around to start a fire.

The Rabbi was sitting by himself, meditating or praying. The well water was bitter, as it often is in the desert, and besides, the Salt Sea was not far away. What could be the prayer or meditation that so absorbed him? The bright sky to the west hadn't quite gone dark, but on the opposite side, above the hilltops, the stars were starting to rise.

I went to lie down some distance away, wrapped in my mantle, a strip of rough grass for a pillow. The wind carried the piercing cries of hungry jackals. Our Eternal God be praised, I murmured, but no prayer took shape in me, my mind was too tired. I hadn't slept well for a long time, and temptations and doubts, hopes and disappointments, had finally exhausted me.

I woke up to see that the winter stars had already set, the summer stars were over my head, bright and cold. The fire near the well was going. Surely, they were sleeping around it, the Rabbi among them. The Eternal made man upright,

I said to myself with Qoheleth, but men have sought out many inventions. I knew something about that myself. But neither did the Eternal seem so comprehensible to the human mind. What need did he have of our labors, searching, complicity, and collaboration? With one gesture, he could have annihilated the empire of Rome, or taken us back to the garden of Eden, with just a word, procure us the goods that would last for an eternity of eternities. Lord, You are Your Name, You alone on all the earth the Most High, but protect us from trials that are too cruel. So I managed to pray before falling asleep.

When I opened my eyes again it was late, the sun already warm. I was alarmed to think that perhaps they had already gone—and I also thought an instant later: so much the better that they've gone—but they were still there, and they hadn't let the fire go out. I wasn't afraid of them. Rabbi, I would have said, I am waiting for the Lord to give me a sign of his might, or of his vanity; what do You say?

But the Rabbi was nowhere to be seen. The others were gathered around the fire, roasting a hare, or maybe a rabbit. There were nine of them, of all ages, the oldest had white hair and red eyes. "Will you give me something to eat? I can pay."

They looked me over, not without mistrust. Finally, the oldest gestured that I could sit down. I crouched down next to one of them who made room for me. We looked at the fire and nobody talked. "Where is the Rabbi?" I asked.

It seemed like nobody wanted to answer me, then the old man said: "The spirit, descended unto him from heaven, has led him into the desert."

"Alone?"

"He didn't want anyone to go with him."

So, the most likely prophet that I had encountered had gone away to interrogate and die. The Eternal is silence.

The rabbit, or hare, was ready. We gave thanks to the Lord and ate in silence, meager portions with a gamey taste. I said in a loud voice: "He mustn't die, Israel today is in need of its best sons."

The old man replied in a subdued tone, "He will not die because our eternal God has descended in him."

"How long have you known him?"

"Seven days ago, he passed through Nain. He looked at me and I followed him. Them too. He looks at you, and you leave everything and walk behind him."

Yes, this was possible. I had seen the power of his eyes, even though they were not looking at me. "How long will he be away?"

"He didn't say."

"What will he eat?"

"He doesn't need to eat. Anyway, in the heavens there is someone who looks after him."

So, all I could do was wait, power or vanity. Together we gave thanks to the Eternal for the food we had eaten. They did not want any money. They said they would be compensated in other ways.

I went off by myself, to meditate.

23

A week went by and two of them left, toward Jerusalem. They were young and they were hungry. There was a lot of fulminating against them by the other seven, but the next night another one left.

I was now sleeping together with them, next to the fire that we kept going, and we woke up at the slightest sound, suspicious, not that the Rabbi was coming back, but that someone else was leaving. The nights were now bathed in moonlight, and if a place was empty, we cast a gaze toward Jerusalem, even the old man who probably couldn't see anymore, his eyelids were so swollen. I asked him, "Do you think he is the Anointed?"

"He who comes from heaven is above all others," he replied.

I rebutted, irritated, "Don't play games with words. Do you believe he is the Anointed or not?"

He walked away and left me without an answer.

There were four of us left. One, whose name was Etai, said, "It's not easy to figure out. Some insist that he is good, others that he deceives people."

Etai was an expert hunter of mice and lizards, which we then ate, giving thanks to the Eternal. The second night after the full moon, he waited until the moon rose above the hills, then he walked off, saying he was going to hunt down a hedgehog whose den he had discovered. He didn't come back.

There were three of us left, then two, myself and the old man with his eyes opaque with trachoma, neither of us able to procure food. "Do you believe that the Rabbi is the Anointed?" I asked him.

"The Name knows," he answered.

Before nightfall he left, too, tripping over the rocks, but toward the desert, not toward Jerusalem.

Why did the Eternal look for such useless victims? I stretched out on the ground, wrapped in my cloak, without tending to the fire that was now going out. O Adonai God Tzebaòt, what are you doing with my youth? With my arrogance and impatience? With my generous vigor?

There was no answer. The stars had no meaning in their closed designs. Better is the end of a thing than the beginning thereof, I told myself with Qohelet, and there is also a time to die.

The next day, some merchants passed by on their way from Jerusalem to the land of the Persians, and they stopped to let their camels drink. They sold me some bread, cheese, and olives. They also gave me some news of the world, even though I didn't ask for any. The tetrarch Herod had ordered the arrest of a false prophet named John, who preached his condemnation for the wife he had taken from his brother.

They said to me, "Times are getting tough for prophets. You're young, why don't you go back home?"

They understood only the young.

24

The Rabbi came at noon, after the fortieth day, his gaze afire as though from fever but his majesty intact, and no thinner or weaker than he had been when he left. He looked around, searching perhaps, though without showing surprise at their absence, or my presence. It was as though he already knew that he would find me there, but it might also have been that I was of no importance to him, that he could look right through my person as valueless.

I tried to provoke him, "They've all gone, days ago now."

He said, "It will happen to me again. It's a bitterness to which it is better that I become accustomed." His voice was appropriate to him; not intense like his gaze, but full of knowing and flattery. It too grabbed hold of you.

I said to him, "If you are looking for followers, I will follow you. As you can see, I alone have waited for you, and you had not called me."

He didn't answer. Was he thinking about my proposal, or was he thinking about something else, as though my proposal had no meaning for him? I tried to provoke him again, "John, the one who baptized you at the river, has been taken by the tetrarch."

He was shaken, and he posed his gaze on me. Did he think I was lying? I was upset and I hurried to explain myself: "Some merchants on their way to the East told me about it. I bought some food from them. Do you want some bread, cheese, olives?"

The sun was hot and he chose a spot to sit down in the shadow of a tree. We gave thanks. Even the gesture of bringing the food to his mouth, and chewing it, was regal in him. He didn't even think about the taste of the food. He said, "The time is near, but it has not yet come. It's best that I return to Galilee."

He had spoken as though he were talking to himself, ignoring my presence.

"Rabbi, why don't you look at me? You looked at the others. I am no less worthy than the others and I am here."

He looked at me, but his gaze bore no signs of invitation or command. His eyes, however, were inquisitive. Perhaps he was trying to understand what my strength was. Then he stood up and started off. I walked beside him.

He must not have been pleased. After a few minutes, exasperated, without looking at me and accelerating his pace, he said to me in a harsh voice, "If one comes to me and does not detest his father and mother, and his wife and siblings, and even his own life, he cannot be my disciple."

I detested even him. "Rabbi," I said to him, "do you think I would be following you if I did not detest myself to the point of wanting to die? But one has to die for something, and you have to tell me, are you the Anointed who will liberate our people or are we to wait for someone else?"

My words irritated him, and he started walking even faster. It was hard for me to keep up with him; I looked like a beggar. "Rabbi, if you are the Anointed, why don't you reveal yourself?"

He stopped cold, aiming a glance at me that was at once painful and aggressive, "Who do you think I am?"

I didn't have an answer. But I didn't fear him. Even though it was beyond measure, I could feel the force of his spirit. I said, "My arm can raise a sword and my spirit is bold. For a king I will fight to the death."

His gaze remained fixed on me, inquisitive and binding. Then, when he had judged me internally, he said, "You cannot imagine the cross that you will be called to bear. When I am in need of death, I will say so."

25

So, I had been welcomed, albeit not very warmly. He began walking again, and I by his side, with anger, exultation, and still impatience. Why must the ways of the Lord be so twisted? Why is this Rabbi so closed and distant?

"Walk a few paces behind me," he said, without even looking at me. "I like to think while I'm walking."

He had put me in my place. If he was not the Anointed that I was waiting for, who was he? Elias? A prophet? Or an emanation of Beelzebub? Anyway, by now I had put my life in his hands.

Night fell and we continued walking in the dark. He seemed to know the paths well. Then again, hadn't he just survived forty days in the desert? We made a long detour to avoid entering Hesbon, land of the sons of Ruben, and even afterwards, when barking dogs and the acrid smell of goats and the stench of pigs alerted us that we were near a village, he became wary, and avoided entering. Surely, he was worried that he might be arrested.

A last-quarter moon rose late and made the walking easier. The desert was finished; the wind made noise among the trees and bushes, the air was perfumed with mint and rosemary.

Then he stopped, listening. He said to me, "Go ahead, you'll come to a village of a few houses around a well. Draw some water and bring me to drink. If anyone says anything to you, tell them it's for Jesus of Nazareth, but don't reveal where I am."

I did as he had ordered, amid insistent barking of dogs, but without anyone coming out to say anything to me. He took a long drink from the gourd with which I had brought him the water. He said, "I think we can sleep here, there's no danger."

He lay down wrapped in his cloak, a rock for a pillow. I did the same, a few steps away. He didn't fall asleep right away. After a few minutes he said to me, "You must know that I am a tough man; I take what I have not put up, and I harvest what I have not sown."

I implored him, "Rabbi, don't speak in enigmas. Are you the Anointed?"

He pondered before answering, and said, "The Anointed is, but he cannot reveal himself if he is not completed by everyone."

He involved you, bound you, demanded of you; in exchange he offered toughness.

I fell asleep as the sky was brightening in the east and the roosters in the village had already been crowing for some time.

I woke up to cheerful laughter. The day was well along; with him were some children, who had brought him a basket of eggs. He said, "Children are dear to me; they are the closest to my father."

We walked all day, toward Galilee, where neither Caesar's soldiers nor Herod's guards went to arrest patriots and prophets.

He in the lead, I a few paces behind. Power or vanity?

26

So I, of the twelve who have been so talked about, and are talked about, was the first. It is true that it was not You who called me, with a word, a glance, or a nod, but I who offered myself. Caught between uncertainty and passion, I was nonetheless obstinate in my purpose, and You, with some perplexity and reluctance, accepted me. In truth, it was not just anyone who could have done what You would ask me to do.

You came from the desert. After forty days of fasting, You had won Your struggle with Satan, it is true, but it is also written that after tempting You in every possible way, the Evil One took his leave of You until another occasion. What occasion? And would You have been able to win again by Yourself?

I said to You, "Rabbi, take me, for a king I will give my life."

And You, knowing that it was death we were talking about, welcomed my prayer.

The others, however, were called by You, it is not known how casually, and in any case their cross was not to be so heavy, not right away anyway. You began with Simon and his brother Andrew, fishermen on Lake Tiberias. The fishing was not going at all well for them, so You said to them, "Follow me, and I will make you fishers of men."

They left their nets and joined us.

Then it was the turn of James and John, sons of Zebedee, fishermen they too, partners with Simon in the ownership of the boat. They were rearranging their nets when You called them, and immediately they left their father and their nets, and came with us.

Then You called others, and still others, and they all came, and I, still doubtful, wondered if vanity could manifest itself with the signs of power. You stopped to talk at cross-roads, next to wells, in the marketplaces and in village synagogues. You performed some easy prodigies, a lot of people believed in You, and You acquired authority with them.

You would say, "Get ready because the coming of the Kingdom is near." You called them to hope, exhorted them to expectation, and what You did was good.

Later, when Your interests became broader in scope and it was opportune to acquire authority beyond the circle of the humble, You, with Your arm outstretched and Your index finger raised—a gesture of regal imperium—called the tax collector Levi who followed You from then on, and on the night of his calling he gave a dinner in Your honor, and the guests included his colleagues who, like him, collected taxes for the Romans, and many of the Pharisees—they were base and envious—criticized You because You sat at table with men who had sold out to the enemy of our people, but You, who believed that even tax collectors were children of God, answered them with words from the Book—I desire compassion and not sacrifices—and You added that You had not come to call those who were already with us but people from the outside, and surely, You had a plan in

Your head: for the imminent struggle supporters were needed not so much from among those who would have been on our side anyway, but among those who, when the moment came for action, might have otherwise taken up sides with the enemy.

And this too was good, of that which You did.

27

Then it happened that the group of followers became too numerous, and it was necessary to make a selection, establish order and a hierarchy, so there would not be any confusion when it was time to act, when it is good to know who is in command, and who has to obey. Therefore, You went to the top of a hill and after spending the whole night questioning our Eternal God—You called him father and You taught us a prayer to recite together: our father who art in heaven—You went back down to the crowd that not without anxiety was waiting for You, and with firmness You named those elected, one by one.

First Simon, later called Peter, second Andrew his brother, then the other two brothers James and John—You already loved John and You would love him even more, he who when he speaks of me calls me a thief—and Philip and Bartholomew and Levi, the tax collector, whose name would become Matthew, and Thomas, and James son of Alphaeus, and Thaddeus, and Simon, who like me had been with the zealots before following You. Eleven You had called, and somehow it was known that there had to be twelve—twelve the tribes of Israel. One was missing, and the twelfth could not be but me—who could have done what I could do?—but You hesitated, perhaps because of John, who detested me.

In the end, without looking either at John or at me, You said, "Judas, son of Simon."

And I, looking at You, said loudly, "My gaze into Yours, Anointed, O Lord."

But Your gaze did not meet mine.

28

So I, who had been the first to follow You, to offer You death and life, was named last, and last I always am when the twelve are listed, the apostles. I am the outcast, he who later betrayed You.

In effect, though living with the group, I kept to myself. I was different, I had not suffered poverty except by choice. I knew the Law and Scripture, while they were coarse and ignorant, with the exception of John, perhaps, handsome and elevated by his ambition. He was very young, still almost a boy. He must have intuited the unspoken pact between us, and he detested me right away. But would he have had my capacity?

You also left me apart. You neglected me. Only when You were taken by thoughts of death—the presentiment of the last hour, mystery, and anguish—then only Your eyes, with a quick glance, sought me out, and I answered You with my eyes that I was ready for the call. I would not back down.

So it came to pass; I did not back down. But objectively, what need was there of betrayal? Why did certain prophecies have to be born out? And I, hanged from a branch? You, Your death, the death that You wanted, You could have achieved without difficulty or complicity, if it was only Your death that You wanted. But what other commitment, or necessity, was in Your mind, Rabbi, or in Your heart, that involved and bound everyone? And, apart from those who abandoned You, who failed to perform as planned? Me? You? The father?

I arrived at my tree questioning myself and questioning the Eternal. Even then, there was no response, and what I did out of desperation is judged unworthy of mercy.

But You, Rabbi, You know: I did what I could do. I had no messengers from the Lord on my side, I was just a man.

29

In Galilee, far from Herod's guards and Rome's soldiers, he began his mission, addressing himself to the poor, the humiliated, the unhappy, to all those who with greater resignation put up with injustices and domination, to set afire within them a hope—the kingdom is nigh—that would make them aware of their strength, of the possibility for change.

He knew how to speak of love with amazing simplicity. Love thy neighbor as thyself was his unceasing exhortation, and little did it matter that it was already in the Book, he pronounced it with a new vigor, he made it into a commandment, and the people, if not persuaded, were at least struck by it, and were able to imagine a rebirth of the faith, a return to the greatness of the fathers, when Israel accomplished great feats, with the sword of the Eternal.

Thy kingdom come, they prayed.

Publicly, in the streets, in the markets, in the synagogues, along the caravansaries, when we met up with groups of wayfarers, he admonished, consoled, incited: change your lives, love one another, stand united, blessed are they who weep for they will be consoled.

Once, but in a voice so low that very few heard him—and nobody understood—he said, "I am the light of the world."

After the baptism, the fasting in the desert, and the victory over Satan, he felt himself to be in the fullness of the spirit. Occasionally, almost against his will, he performed some prodigy, cripples and demoniacs mostly, as so many other prophets less likely than he had done, but his power had longer effect, never did we face the misadventure of having to run away to escape insults, clubbing, or stoning.

Until he got the bright idea of going back to Nazareth.

30

Nazareth of Galilee was the modest village where he had grown up and from where he had come away not so long ago, perhaps thinking then that he would not set foot there again anytime soon. What led him back there: exhibitionism, a sense of superiority, romantic illusion or, who knows, impatience?

We arrived there—I was his only follower, still—one Friday when it was already dark, and he did not want to go to his parents' house. We took refuge in a cave and spent most of the night praying, not together but each on his own. I, as always, asked the Eternal for a sign that would help me understand whether that Rabbi, whose following I had joined with such good will, was the Anointed, or just any ordinary prophet, or a rogue like the many rogues that were then roaming the lands of Israel, only a little less roguish. There were no signs.

The next morning, we recited the prayer together—our father who art in heaven, they kingdom come—then he started off resolute—and I behind him—toward the center of the village for the ceremony of the Sabbath. Everyone knew him, and naturally he knew everyone, but he didn't look at anybody. He saw an empty seat and took it, remaining for a time collected.

Then, as though overcome with inspiration, he suddenly stood up, asked the person in charge for the book of the prophet Isaiah, opened the scroll, and quickly found a passage to read. Now he was serene, firm, solemn, his youthful beauty stood out in the midst of that community of peasants, shepherds, tradesmen, from which for better or worse he himself had come, only to take, who knows how, another road.

He let the right amount of time go by, then read in a slow, even-pitched voice, without a hint of condescension, as though he were reading something quite ordinary. "The Spirit of the Lord is upon me; because he hath anointed me to preach good tidings unto the meek; he hath sent me to bind up the brokenhearted, to restore sight to the blind, to proclaim liberty to the captives, and the opening of the prison to them that are bound. To proclaim the welcome year of the Lord."

When he was finished reading, he rolled up the scroll, gave it back to the person in charge, went back to his seat from before, and sat there, firm in his majesty. The people gazed at him in amazement, but also with puzzlement, asking themselves what this all meant.

I too was asking myself. In saying liberty for the captives, was he also thinking of the Baptist, who was then a prisoner in Herod's jail? And the sight that he meant to restore to the blind, was it limited to a few prodigies, or did it have a broader value, such as making things understood to those who were not able to understand them on their own? And the liberation of those who are bound, could that also have meant something more than could be understood literally? And the welcome year of the Lord, was it legitimate to think of it as something different than the time of our liberation from the infidels?

He always spoke in that way, binding those who listened to him to the duty of interpretation, and at times also to an obscure commitment.

31

But the people in the synagogue of Nazareth didn't seem to find any satisfying interpretations, and as regards commitments, they preferred to keep their distance. They looked at one another inquisitively, asked questions and made comments under their breath, and the buzzing kept growing louder.

He didn't let it get out of control. He raised a hand, and when he had them all quiet and attentive, he said with solemnity, "Today, this passage from the Scripture has become true, as you have heard."

His solemnity, even more than his words, was intended to make them understand that he had been given a great and special charge from our Eternal God, with authority to announce, liberate, heal, and the people, as simple as they were, had understood well what he wanted to make them understand, but they didn't appear to accept it. They went back to murmuring, between scandal and amazement. What impudence! Isn't he the son of Joseph the carpenter? And isn't his mother Mary, Siba's daughter? And aren't his brothers named James, Joshua, Judas, and Simon? And don't his sisters make dough, light the oven, go to the well right here in our midst? What is he trying to do, trick us into something, put one over on us?

The Rabbi felt the aversion rising up against him and it didn't scare him, but then his face flushed with anger, and he said forcefully, "You surely have heard that I speak words of truth and perform prodigies. I have also spoken words of truth to you, but I will not perform prodigies for you because you have not received me well. It is well known that a prophet is not without honor save in his own country, among his family, and in his own house. But verily I say to you, I have been chosen."

On hearing these words said almost as a challenge, his countrymen were infuriated, and they stood up and grabbed him and threw him out of the synagogue. They dragged him to the edge of the precipice, on which the village was built, and they wanted to throw him down, or practically, considering the height of the drop, to kill him. He let them proceed, posed no opposition to the violence. It appeared that he intended to let them have the full responsibility for whatever might happen. It was hard to tell if his attitude was indicative of residual or new magnificence, or if he had totally lost the majesty that usually shone brilliantly in him. Be that as it may, he continued to let them act unimpeded, and so he took on more and more the appearance of a poor soul like the many I had already seen. In my view, however, he remained the least unlikely prophet I had happened upon, and it pained me to see him come to such a horrible end. But what could I do, by now they were ready to throw him over the cliff.

But instead, he managed to raise his right hand and shoot back at them a vexed stare in which all of his majesty appeared once again, and they let him go immediately, ceased their violence, stood there looking at him in awe, even with submission. And, like a king recovering from a small incident, he walked through the middle of the crowd, taking his leave.

I followed him, naturally; one who possessed that kind of power was capable of doing great things for the cause of an oppressed people.

32

He didn't say a word as we left Nazareth behind us on the way to Capernaum, on the shores of Lake Tiberias. His rage passed, and the act of imperium completed, he was engulfed with a deadly sadness and immeasurable dejection. Whatever the hoped-for fruits of his return to his hometown, I was still his only follower.

I dared to approach him. "Rabbi, you are right, the most difficult to convince are those of your own home. But your words were just. I believe you have come for the liberation of our oppressed people."

He meditated for several minutes on what I had said to him—perhaps it was something removed from what he was thinking at that moment—then he gestured with his head to indicate that I should keep my distance, and I obeyed. He was a tough man; he had told me so. But we were in need of men like him if we wanted to vanquish Rome.

33

In Capernaum things changed for the better right away, there was no preconceived mistrust, the people were favorably disposed to listen to what he had to say. All week long, we walked through the countryside or along the lakeshore, and he stopped to talk to fishermen, farmhands, vinedressers, shepherds, and he always found the right words to console them and exhort them to cooperate, to love one another, and remain united until the coming of the kingdom. On the Sabbath, he taught in the synagogue, and the people were struck by his teaching, because he spoke with authority.

One Saturday, there in the synagogue in Capernaum, he took the risk of performing a rather sensational prodigy. It went really well for him too, considering that Capernaum is not so far from Nazareth to allow one to think that the people did not know that the man called Jesus of Nazareth was the son of a carpenter named Joseph and a woman just like most of the women who lived in Capernaum, so that, even putting aside the ill repute of Nazareth, it could not but appear a bit excessive that he, beyond preaching with authority and suggesting, as soon as they gave him the opportunity, that he was indeed the promised Anointed of the Lord—but in reality he was not the only one to proclaim himself the Anointed in the Palestine of those times—that he also set about performing prodigies, and not furtively, but right there, for everybody to see.

In effect, that Saturday the synagogue was very crowded and there was great anticipation for him—he knew how to make people desire his appearance and nobody ever knew where we slept: in a hay loft, an abandoned barn, in the bottom of a boat pulled up on the shore—and when he finally appeared, everybody became tense and reverent. He was on his way to the raised step from which he usually preached when suddenly, a man with the spirit of an impure demon started shouting at the top of his lungs—and it was, clearly, Satan who was shouting through his mouth: "Go away, Jesus of Nazareth, You have nothing in common with us; You have come to destroy us. You can do it because You are the holy one of the Lord."

It was a wonderful, and truthful, testimonial, but it came from an impure spirit, and he could not accept it. Therefore, overcome with majestic rage, and speaking directly to the demon who was inside the man, he ordered it, "Be silent, and leave the body of this man!"

And the demon, furious and impotent, managed to throw to the ground the unfortunate man that he possessed, but was then forced to leave him without doing any harm.

Everyone in the synagogue was amazed and frightened, and they said to one another, "What is happening? He gives orders, with force, to impure spirits, and those spirits, humiliated, obey him?"

Things that were later recounted around the area and his fame spread throughout the region.

34

Day by day, we were getting stronger; the numbers of those who believed in him were growing. He had already called Simon, later known as Peter, and his brother Andrew, and he had called James and his brother John, young and handsome among the sons of man, treacherous and ambitious. More and more new followers flocked to join us, avid to hear him speak, anxious to be present for some extraordinary feat.

And it was in the house of Simon Peter, on one of those days, that he performed one of his most predictable prodigies when, having come there for dinner, he found Simon's mother-in-law in the grip of an extremely high fever, and since they begged him to do something, he, leaning down over her, threatened the fever, and the fever left her, and she, having immediately gotten out of bed, began to serve us.

This feat, immediately known outside the house—and perhaps someone took it upon himself to make it known even sooner—provoked gossip and wonder in the town. Was he able to command even fever? So it was, the incredulous were silenced.

Meanwhile, the sun was setting. At that hour, people were used to retiring to their homes to sleep, but there was too much ferment, curiosity, hope in the town, and those who had someone ill or incapacitated in the family, whatever the malady might be that affected them, ran to Simon's house to present them to him, and he, spreading his hands over each of them, healed them.

For the most part, they were demoniacs, whose evil spirit, perceiving the proximity of Jesus, began to shout, "Be gone! You vanquish us! You are the Anointed, the son of God in the flesh!"

The Rabbi threatened them, he didn't let them go on shouting that way—but in the meantime they had shouted as much as they wished—and they, the evil spirits, were forced to leave. There was a flow of people until late at night, and in the end, we were all so tired we slept there.

35

He woke us before daybreak, and we set off for more peaceful places.

When the townspeople realized that we had left, they ran after us; they wanted to take possession of him so that he would stay with them and teach and heal. When they caught up with us, they surrounded him, grabbed ahold of his clothing; they wanted to keep him from going.

But the Rabbi, who had already sown enough seed in that region, said, "I need to go to announce the kingdom of God in other places, because that is what I was sent to do."

He had surely achieved success, and he went off to preach in the synagogues of Judea. Only a few of us followed him: Peter and Andrew, James and John, and myself, though I was never clearly invited, always kept at a distance. Nevertheless, each morning, as we were about to leave again, when, partly on purpose, I showed myself uncertain, almost hesitant about whether to go with them or not, there was a moment when his gaze asked me to follow him, and I followed him, in obedience, bemoaning in my heart the time when it was I alone who followed him, albeit at a distance.

Now there was Peter, coarse but destined to command, and there was John, destined for predilection. I detested him more all the time, John, as he detested me. Nevertheless, we were both conscious of the fact that when you hate you don't hate just anyone, and that hate is a turbid blend of things, one of which is love. It was he, the Rabbi, who somehow held us together.

Together we made our way along the roads, the trails, and the footpaths of Galilee, Samaria, and Judea, the Rabbi with his intimates, and I a few paces behind, perhaps not an intimate, but obscurely necessary. He preached, taught, performed easy and nebulous prodigies, and the number of those who threw in to follow him quickly grew larger. At that point, he would leave them, warning them to be ready for the imminent hour, and go on to a new place, always accompanied by his most faithful. With us now were also Matthew, Bartholomew, Simon the zealot, and others, and each of us did all he could to strengthen his mission.

With immeasurable authority, he promised, admonished, threatened, and manifested himself by performing prodigies, winning over followers in huge numbers. He was, more and more, the probable redeemer, the liberator of Israel.

36

There are forms of love that are boundless—when the love is for an ideology—and nevertheless prudent—when the ideology is incarnated—the word made flesh. I had offered to die for You, at any moment You should have asked me I would have maintained my promise. I often dreamed that You would ask me on the spot so I could prove my devotion to You, but, as soon as I could, I looked on You with suspicion.

You were not easy; a tangle of contradictions, of conflicts. You knew that You were tough and sweet—tough with me, but so sweet with children, and with John, who was little more than a child—obscure and limpid—You spoke to the people only in parables, then in private You explained everything to us, often the explanations were more impenetrable than the parables—exhibitionist and reserved—You incited the crowds to admire You, to yearn for You, then You suddenly disappeared, You withdrew to the desert or You escaped with a boat that You had ordered us to keep always ready so the crowd would not smother You—law abiding and at the same time a rebel. One day You said, while boldly teaching a freedom that not all of Your followers over the centuries have known well enough: the Sabbath is made for man and not man for the Sabbath. On the one hand, You feared the Pharisees and You tried in various ways to appease them. On the other, You provoked and insulted them. You used to say that the commandments are to be respected—including honor thy father and mother, as our Eternal God commanded You—but You, how many times were You rude, if not downright offensive, to Your mother and Your family. The latter deserved it, but Your mother?

You took John with You to the wedding feast at Cana and he later wrote what happened. They had run out of wine halfway through the banquet, and to Your mother who asked You to do something, You responded rudely: "What have I to do with thee, woman? My hour has not yet come."

Then the prodigy—that bizarre prodigy—You performed it anyway, but Your response to Your mother was tough.

It's a fact that with Your siblings You had rather rancorous relationships, almost as though among yourselves the commandment to love one another was given short shrift. Strange things happened in Your family.

To begin with, that ugly day in Nazareth, when You nearly ended up at the bottom of the cliff, why weren't Your brothers in the synagogue to back You up against the hostile crowd? Or were they actually there, but they didn't make themselves seen or heard? Couldn't it be that they thought that Your death would rid them of a lot of troubles? You were the restless brother, with too many fantasies filling Your head, and very little desire to work, and because of You a lot of people blamed the whole family.

37

The time came when Your success grew beyond measure, throngs of demoniacs continually threw themselves at Your feet, shouting that You were the son of God, and You, vexed, threatened them, not wanting those words to come from their mouths. Nevertheless, You freed them from their demons. Crowds followed You, not only Galileans, but also Judeans, even from Jerusalem itself they came, and from Edom and from the other side of the Jordan, and from the region of Tyre and Sidon—even infidels, therefore, people who lived in the Greek way. One day, in a village not far from Nazareth, You found Yourself under a sort of siege in a house; a multitude of fanatics who wanted to see You, touch You, take You away with them, they pressured You with such insistence that You couldn't even eat.

In the midst of all those people there were also doctors of law, come for a firsthand assessment, and other people sent to evaluate the size of the movement, and still others who deviously provoked incidents to give the authorities a pretext to intervene and, all in all, the chaos was huge and not without danger, and when Your family heard about it, they were frightened, they thought it was their duty to get You out of there, maybe even by force, and they went around saying that You were mad, Your head wasn't right they said, and maybe they weren't totally sincere in affirming that, but being outside the house and not being able to get in, they could easily have thought that the situation was more dangerous than it actually was, with those doctors of law from Jerusalem proclaiming in loud voices that You had an unclean spirit within You, that You exorcized demons in cahoots with Beelzebub the prince of demons. So there was a risk that the cheering masses would become—at the drop of a hat, as often happens—persecuting masses, and, all things considered, saying that You were mad in those circumstances—the shouting of the demoniacs, the hosannas of the miraculously healed, the protests of the doctors of law, the unruly crowd—could even appear to be a more or less acceptable way to get You out of trouble. But what was the true spirit with which they were doing all this? Were they to be trusted? Were You already aware that they would be capable of betraying You?

That day, in any event, not succeeding by any means in entering the house, they sent a messenger to tell You that Your mother and Your brothers were outside, and they wanted You.

But You, turning Your gaze to us who were sitting around the table with You, said, "Behold my mother and my brothers, because the one who will have done God's will, that one is my brother, my sister, my mother."

And You didn't go to them.

Was this a new concept—enlarged, universal—of the family, or was it that You just couldn't bear to see them?

It seems that You had good reasons not to trust them.

38

John recounts that You didn't feel comfortable going around Judea because the Judeans were trying to eliminate You. Everybody knew that.

Now the Feast of the Tabernacles, which was celebrated in Jerusalem in memory of the migrations in the desert, was near. Therefore, Your brothers said to You, "Leave and go to Judea, so that the Judeans will also see the works that You do. If You wish to be publicly recognized, show Yourself to the world."

"Not even his brothers believed in him," John comments bitterly. And he reports the response that You gave them, more disconsolate than irritated, "My time has not yet come. Your time, on the other hand, is always ready. The world cannot hate you, but it hates me, because I testify that its works are evil. You go up to the feast. I shall not go to this feast because my time has not yet fully come."

Then, however, You went, but after letting Your brothers leave, and as though in a hidden way.

Rabbi, if the betrayal was inevitable, why did You not serve Yourself of one of them? They didn't believe in You. Neither did I believe, then, but I loved You, asking myself always why it was easier to love You than to believe in You.

39

Love one another, You taught us, but You warned us that to be one of Yours we had to hate and hate ourselves, not have weaknesses.

"Follow me and let the dead bury their dead," You responded to a disciple who, on learning that his father had died, asked You for permission to go bury him.

Your fury was majestic like the ire of the Most High. One day, there was an epileptic boy and, in Your absence, some of us attempted to heal him—You had given us permission to do so—but without success.

When You came back, the father of the boy addressed himself to You, "Rabbi, I brought You my son who has a mute spirit. Every so often it takes possession of him, and he froths and gnashes his teeth and goes stiff. I told Your disciples to exorcise the spirit but they were not able to."

You were immediately overcome with fury, and without our understanding whether You were angry with us for not succeeding in performing the miracle—it was a special demon, You explained later—or with all of those present in general, You shouted, "O faithless and perverse generation! How long shall I be with you? How long shall I suffer you?"

I liked Your fury, I could imagine it unleashed against the infidels.

The day that You realized that some of the villages where You had performed the largest number of prodigies had not changed at all but kept on living in sin the same or worse than before, You burst out in vociferous invective, raging even at Capernaum, where they had welcomed You benignly, after You had had to escape from Nazareth. You shouted, "You, Capernaum, what fate shall be yours? Shall you be exalted unto heaven? No, you shall be brought down to Hell! If the mighty works that have been done in thee had been done in Sodom, today that city would still exist. I declare that on the Day of Judgment, Sodom shall be treated less severely than you!"

Unfathomable, like the designs of Adonai God of Israel.

You would say, with flattery, "Become my disciples, because I do not impose myself with violence and in my heart I am close to the humble."

But one day, when You announced that You would be going to Jerusalem, where You would find much suffering and death, and Peter, who was not only humble but also quite fearful, started to urge You not to go, You were overcome with rage—or was it an instance of masking insecurity?—and You inveighed against him, "Get thee behind me, Satan, for thou savorest not the things of God, but the things of men."

Yet, not long before that, in Caesarea Philippi, it having come to Your mind to provoke us by asking—aggressive, subtle, and in some way amused: "What do the people say I am?" Peter spoke up immediately to answer for us all, "You are the Anointed, the son of the living God!"

And You, content, instantly named him head of the whole community of Your faithful on earth.

40

For me, however, it was always less than certain that You were the Anointed, the Promised, the Awaited. With all my will, I strove to believe it, but I couldn't, without a sign from the Eternal, or from You.

The signs that You gave, the prodigies, were not enough for me. And yet I loved You, much more than John loved You, boundlessly. In Your uncertainty and fear, as in Your resoluteness and courage, in Your meekness and in Your fury, in Your tenacious melancholy and in Your brief smiles, and more in Your delusions of grandeur, I loved You.

You would say, submissively, "I am the light of the world."

Or also, "Everything that the father has is mine."

Then my soul too was delirious, in a summit of identification, because You were that which I had not been able to be, and I wanted to be one with You.

Those were the moments in which I most intensely wanted You to call me, to enjoy immediately that communion of death that was our pact.

41

But it was enchantment, not faith, and there remained a whole sphere of things that were murky, in which I felt that You were ambiguously trying to involve us—even I who, enchanted, put up no resistance—for a purpose that still had too many veils of mystery.

One day, in that same synagogue in Capernaum, You began to teach: "Verily, I say to you, unless you eat the flesh of the son of man and drink his blood, you have no life in you. Who so eats my flesh and drinks my blood has eternal life and I will raise him up on the last day. For my flesh is true meat and my blood is true drink. He who eats my flesh and drinks my blood dwells in me and I in him."

Who could understand You? But all the same I was delirious, in the ardor of the thought that You should dwell in me, and I in You, whatever that might mean.

The others, however, remained distant; they looked at one another bewildered, asked each other questions, murmured.

You preferred to ignore them and—For me? For me alone?—You continued: "As the living father hath sent me, and I live by the father, so he that eats me, even he shall live by me. This is that bread which came down from heaven, not that which was eaten by your now dead fathers. He that eats of this bread shall live forever."

I was still afire with Your greatness, but the others mur-mured louder and louder, many opined that what You had said was unacceptable, that one could not stand to listen to such raving. To the point that You could no longer ignore their dissent, and You said, not in anger, but rather with moderation, and a sense of distress: "Does this seem absurd to you? And if you were to see the son of man ascend to where he was before? It is the spirit that quickens, the flesh profits nothing. The words that I have spoken to you are spirit and life."

Quickened by the spirit, I drank down Your words one by one as You pronounced them, until You concluded: "But among you there are some who believe not."

42

My exultation ceased at once; indeed, I did not believe. "No man can come to me unless it is given to him by my father," You said, and the Lord had still not given me a sign, I had to come to You by other ways.

But I did not go away when those who did not believe left. You counted us, those who remained—we were twelve—and almost as a challenge—but surely You wanted to underline that staying with You required an unceasing surrender—You apostrophized us: "Will you also go away?"

For everyone, as usual, and promptly, Peter answered: "And to whom should we go? You have words of eternal life and we have believed, and we know that you are the son of the living God."

You fixed Your eyes on Peter, to assure Yourself of his sincerity, then You stared at the other eleven of us, one by one, to see if the profession of faith was valid for us all. You did not linger over anyone in any special way. You displayed no doubts or second thoughts about anyone. You said that everything was fine.

But then, lowering Your gaze to the ground, that is, without looking at me or anyone else, and suddenly overcome with melancholy, You added that among us twelve, there was a devil.

Nobody expected that. In moments of ire it came easy to You to call someone a devil, but in that moment You were not irate, just very sad. The accusation weighed, intolerably, on each of us, because each of us, in the face of Your demands, had his shortcomings. We were afraid to look at one another, and to look at You. Nobody wished to accept the accusation, but neither to lay it on someone else.

Only John. When, many years later, he wrote down this story, he commented, "He alluded to Judas Iscariot, son of Simon, for he, in fact, was about to betray him, and he was one of the twelve."

It's true; I was one of the twelve, and I was about to betray You. But what could John have known about that then? What could he have known about our union and complicity?

He hated me. Yet, of the four who recounted Your life, he was the only one who told the truth with regard to the betrayal.

43

We remained in twelve to follow You, with me more and more on the margins and under suspicion, and nevertheless sustained by the anticipation of my moment.

We started all over again. We went from village to village in Galilee, pushed ourselves beyond Samaria toward Judea—with caution, ready to run for it in case of danger—easily winning over new proselytes. The crowds came to You to listen to Your word, and You spoke splendidly, enchanting them: "Blessed are your eyes for they see, and your ears for they hear. No one before you ever saw what you see or heard what you hear."

You also performed a lot of prodigies, sometimes quite freely, other times reluctantly, never overlooking the effect they would have on the masses. The cause mustn't ever be forgotten.

I, however, was doubtful as always. In the continual overcoming of limits—with each passing day You showed us that the value of Your coming was ever more vast—what importance could be attributed to those prodigies that even others, it wasn't known just how, performed in abundance: demons exorcized by the dozen—one time You transferred an entire legion of them to a drove of pigs, which then threw themselves into the lake, drowning—cripples and the benumbed suddenly made to walk, the blind and dumb healed, and even a woman with menstrual bleeding? Could these really be the manifestations of Your divine might?

But perhaps it was not so much Your might that merited attention, as Your power. The erudite scholars who said that You worked in league with Beelzebub—they said the same thing of many others—never questioned Your power, and it was tempting to think that if Your power came from the evil one, instead of from the Most High, it didn't make much difference, as long as it served to liberate us from our enemies.

However, was it really conceivable that the evil one should work for the salvation of the people of God? Wasn't it more reasonable to suppose that the power abided in You, in Your will, personality, and intelligence, and perhaps in Your cunning?

Often Your prodigies had an air of trickery, complicity, but I had no reason to be scandalized, or to contest them, if they served to win over the masses to the coming kingdom. Your word enchanted, Your gaze instilled submission, Your exploits exacted commitment. Throngs which had not eaten since the day before, suddenly felt satiated, and the word spread that, having available only a few loaves and fishes, You had fed innumerable multitudes. People who were drinking unclean water suddenly had the impression they were drinking excellent wine, and there was a rumor that at a wedding banquet You had transformed five hundred liters of water into wine.

All of this might have been just fine: it served the cause. The hour is coming, and this is it, You preached, and if to convince our people You also performed wondrous prodigies that left doubters with some suspicion as to their authenticity, it mustn't be considered reason for contempt or repulsion.

Perhaps one day the Eternal would reveal himself even through these things, and we would understand, but in the meantime, I often felt bitter and tormented, and I found a friend in the darkness.

44

The darkness continually brought forth new questions. Hadn't the demons transferred to the pigs caused the death of the pigs and damage to their owner and maybe also to their custodian? And what reason could there be to curse and wither a fig tree that didn't have figs in a season that was not the season for figs?

One day we met up with a man who was blind from birth, and they asked You, "Rabbi, why was he born blind? Who sinned, he or his parents?"

You responded that neither he nor his parents had sinned, but that it was necessary that the works of God be manifested in him. Then You granted him sight to show the power of the Lord. But couldn't the power of the Lord have shown itself better by not letting people be born blind? At the origin of Your prodigies there was always an evil; but why the evil?

A resurrection must be preceded by death. The resurrection of Lazarus served to show the power of God over death and over the pain of those who suffered because of it. But what of the infinite other deceased to whom nobody said: arise?

Too many questions, and the Eternal did not respond, nor did the questions find answers within me, nor could I ask them of You; I wouldn't have been able to bear Your anger.

You were painfully unjust, Jesus. One could not come to You unless it was given to him by the father, and You knew that the father would never give it to me to reach You, that I would not eat Your flesh nor drink Your blood if not in amorous delirium. You also knew that I believed not—perhaps I was a demon in the midst of You and Your followers—and yet You kept me subjugated, You made me understand that I had to be ready for more, Your baptism of water, You said, was only the premise for another baptism.

How binding Your insistence on death!

45

Paul later wrote: "Do you not know, perhaps, that all of us who were baptized in Christ were baptized in his death?"

Death was the sign that the Eternal Adonai Tzebaòt attempted to give us through You, in a universal dimension.

Many centuries later, an Austrian Jew, he too the preacher of a new gospel, explained that the delusion of grandeur leads to the negation of everything, to the final solution.

You conceived salvation as glory, and the glory is the reality of the end of time, the immensity of the end of everything, the entering into God, forever and for everyone. The mystery of this just barely touched me when You nebulously spoke of flesh and blood and eternal life. I could feel that You were aiming higher than what was said by Your earthly words, but I didn't know how to follow You, I could only offer You life and death, when You should ask for it.

The kingdom was drawing near, as You preached, and I in my darkness impatiently awaited the time in which it would no longer be necessary to make manifest the works of God.

46

It appeared that the Rabbi, whatever it was he had in mind to prepare, was preparing it confusedly, without any coherent idea, or at least without an established program. He moved around from one place to another at times on a whim, attracted crowds only to send them away, made himself understood and more often misunderstood, spoke of the kingdom as a reality that everyone could see right before their eyes, even touch—the kingdom is already present, he would say at times, but it wasn't easy to perceive—and the next day this kingdom became something that transcended the confines of history and comprehension, the mind couldn't manage to conceive of it.

He had chosen, as trusted and intimate collaborators, people of little account. Of the twelve—if you excluded John and myself—who had a personality? They were ignorant, inept, gossipy, inconstant, envious of one another—as was John of me and I of him—quarreled among themselves to determine who was the best, who could claim the place at the right hand in the kingdom, were easily frightened not only by the hostile attitude of the doctors of law and the Pharisees, or because there were rumors circulating that there were soldiers of Herod nearby, but also by certain unforeseeable prodigies or obscure predictions of the Rabbi.

Nevertheless, little by little, with his teaching, persuasion, invective, threats, he managed to educate them and refine them. He brought forth in them—in us—the conviction, the hope, the suspicion that we were privileged, destined to high undertakings and even higher recompense. "I have given unto you to know the secrets of heaven, but to the others no," he would say, and although no one among them had any idea of the secrets of heaven, they were still content with that privilege.

I, on the other hand, studying them also with regard to other aspects felt discomforted; in the best of cases, they could have become martyrs, or rather victims, never commanders. Not even one of them had an arm as strong as the soldiers of Rome, nor a spirit so proud.

Commanders, nonetheless, we would have found more than enough—there was no zealot who did not believe in his heart that he was a leader—when the people started to move, but they had to start moving, and the only man in Israel capable of getting the people to move was him. If he had given them the order, the crowds would have followed him, without preparation or political awareness, but ready to do whatever he ordered them to do. He had that power, and there were many who knew it.

From Jerusalem, those who wielded power together with the Romans continually sent intellectuals, Pharisees, and spies to see what was happening, and even Herod Antipas, the tetrarch who with Caesar's approval had jurisdiction over Galilee, wanted to be informed of everything and, superstitious as he was, he was very impressed by the prodigies that the Rabbi performed on the demoniacs, and even more so by the persistent rumor that he was the Baptist resurrected.

The tetrarch said to himself: "No one is resurrected from the dead, at least not until the last day, and the Baptist is dead, I saw his head on the plate with my own eyes. But then, who can this subject of mine be, about whom I have received such extraordinary news?"

And he looked for a way to meet him.

47

All of us knew how risky it was to be seen by a monarch who, with a pinch of displeasure and a great deal of composure, cut off the heads of prophets. Our movement was based exclusively on the charismatic power of Jesus of Nazareth, and it would quickly dissolve if they should ever capture him prematurely and put him to death.

He knew it too, and in fact he started taking a few more precautions. As soon as the crowds grew too big, he withdrew from them, disappeared, perhaps only to reappear miraculously where it was least expected, and there were even legends that grew up around this behavior of his.

It happened one day, for example, that Peter and three others were in a boat out in the middle of the lake—they were going to see if they could find some fish for dinner—and suddenly they saw the Rabbi coming toward them on foot, walking on the surface of the water as though it were a lawn, and Peter, who wanted to try it too, almost drowned, and what's more he was given a reprimand because it was exactly owing to his lack of faith that he was unable to stay in the air or walk on water.

The quantity and quality of his prodigies were also calibrated more carefully, as well as the speeches and teachings, which frequently took the form of parables. He must also have been of the opinion that an excessive popularity was not advisable, in that moment, and in fact when Peter, on behalf of everyone, proclaimed that for us he was the Anointed come from God, he severely ordered him not to say anything to anyone.

Maybe it was because of Herod's increasing interest in his person that it was decided to seek friendships outside of Galilee. With the Samaritans—paying little attention to the disapproval of right-minded people—he adopted a cordial attitude toward them and went to perform prodigies in Syro-Phoenician territory, and beyond the Jordan, in the territory of the Decapolis, he performed a prodigy, which was not extraordinary but was executed with extraordinary shrewdness.

That day, there was a huge crowd around us, and they brought him a deaf-mute. Usually, it came extremely easy for him to heal deaf-mutes, and so it was this time too, but he decided not to do it in front of everyone. He took him out of the sight of the crowd and saying, "It is done," he restored him both word and hearing, and then, so healed, he brought him back in front of the crowd and ordered them not to talk about that healing, but he knew that the more he told them not to talk about it the more they actually would.

Anyway, it was good propaganda, in that country inhabited for the most part by gentiles.

48

And the time came when he also decided to make use of us, the twelve, to increase his power. It happened rather strangely.

He called us together to give us some orders and he spoke to us in a tender and melancholy tone, as though his spirit were full of unhappy presentiments, and perhaps lacking in trust in the positive outcome of the things that he was sending us to do.

He began by saying: "You are my friends and you do what I command you to do. I do not call you servants because a servant does not know what his lord does, but I call you friends because all that I have heard from my father I have made known to you. You did not choose me, but I chose you"—as always, I was left out—"and I have ordained you that you should go and bring forth fruit. Whatsoever you shall ask of the father in my name, he shall give it to you. This I command you, that you should love one another."

He paused, and then he gave us detailed instructions: "Now I will send you out among the people. Take nothing for the journey, at most a staff. No bread, nor bag, nor money or belt. Sandals yes, but not two tunics. When you enter a hospitable house, stay there until it is time to leave. But if in some place they do not welcome you and do not listen to you, leave it immediately and shake the dust from your feet as testimony against them. Do not go to pagan lands and do not enter the cities of the Samaritans. Go instead among the lost sheep of the people of Israel. Along the way, proclaim that the kingdom of God is at hand, and heal the sick. I give you my authority over unclean spirits."

He then paused for a longer time, and concluded: "Behold, I am sending you out as sheep among wolves, so be wise as serpents and innocent as doves."

He began to bid us farewell, two by two: Peter and his brother Andrew, James and his brother John, Philip and Bartholomew, Thomas and the tax collector Matthew, James son of Alpheus and Thaddeus. The only two left were Simon the zealot and myself. Simon said: "Rabbi, I do not dare to heal the sick. Grant me to go to Jerusalem."

I said, "Grant it also to me."

He meditated for a moment and said, "The father be with you."

I untied from my belt the purse that held my money and went to place it at his feet.

He said, "Know that the judges are looking for me to kill me, and my disciples will also be persecuted because of me."

49

We walked for three days, and crossing Samaria we did not enter a single village, as we had been ordered. In one way or another we found a way to feed ourselves, field greens and wild fruit, and then there was always somebody—shepherd or farmer or wayfarer—who for love of the god of Israel gave us an egg, or a crust of bread, a piece of cheese or some olives. As the Feast of the Tabernacles was approaching, a lot of people were walking to Jerusalem.

The city would be crowded, and that wasn't bad for Simon and me, since we had to stay hidden from the Romans, and also from the guards of the Temple, if possible. It was very likely that they had been given orders to be on the lookout for Galileans, because of Jesus of Nazareth, but nobody, listening to us, would have taken us for Galileans. In fact, I was Judean, not Galilean, and Simon, having lived for several years in Jerusalem when he was a militant with the zealots, had lost his Galilean accent. Anyway, we knew where to go to be safe.

It was an inn along the street that led to the Temple. The innkeeper, whose name was Aser, was a man of great wisdom: he didn't like the Romans, and when he could, without risk to himself, he helped the zealots, who were regulars at the inn. He was happy to see us. He was also of the opinion that for the next few days, with all those people on the streets, we could stay in Jerusalem at no risk. I asked him for news of Ariel, one of the leaders of the movement.

Ariel didn't come to the inn that often anymore, Aser informed us. He too had irritated the Romans, and he had to look out for himself if he didn't want to end up on Golgotha. Nevertheless, there were ways to let him know of our arrival.

Ariel came in the next evening. He already knew that we were followers of Jesus of Nazareth, and he was anxious to hear what we thought of the man and his movement.

I said to him, "If we want to kick the Romans out of our country, we have to have the people on our side, not only in the cities, but also in the country. No liberation movement can succeed without the support of the people. Jesus of Nazareth has an extraordinary power to get the masses to follow him."

As I was talking, he had a look of skepticism on his face, and he wasn't convinced by what I had to say. Indeed, he responded sourly, "Your Jesus is too meek; he preaches love, forgiveness. When did it ever happen that Israel felt the need to forgive her enemies? His teaching is fine for women. In fact, he has a lot of them among his followers."

I said: Jesus is beautiful among the sons of man, he has majesty in his face and in his feats, fascination in his gaze and voice, and what he says enchants. Women follow him, and so do men, with the same dedication. As for his teaching, I think that if he tells us to love one another and forgive each other, he does it so that the people will be united, he wants the rancor and rivalries that so often divide us, our families and our tribes, to be toned down."

He didn't agree. "His teaching is useless. He takes no account of national unity; he has relationships with

Samaritans and gentiles, even with Romans. Are we supposed to forgive the Romans too?"

That was something I had also asked myself, more than once, never daring to put the question to the Rabbi directly. I replied, "He never mentions the Romans."

Ariel rebutted, ironically, "Right, maybe for him they don't exist, there is no Roman domination over Israel. But we know that one of his prodigies was performed to the benefit of a Roman centurion."

It was true. One day, we were on the road to Capernaum, and we saw an officer coming toward us—a Macedonian by birth but a soldier in the Roman army, on assignment as an advisor to the tetrarch Herod—who was then looking for the Rabbi, asking for help because one of his servants, who was very dear to him, had taken ill and was suffering terribly. That officer, albeit a pagan, had infused his prayer to the Rabbi with so much faith that the Rabbi healed his servant right then and there, without even going to his house, where, in reality, he had never set foot.

I explained this to Ariel, and I also recounted to him what the Rabbi had said to us on that occasion, admonishing us with harsh words, "Many shall come from east and west and they will sit down at the feast with Abraham, Isaac, and Jacob in the kingdom of heaven. But those who were supposed to be at home in the kingdom will be thrown out into the darkness, and there shall be weeping and gnashing of teeth."

He shot back with force, "He's mad. He discourages our brothers of Israel in order to favor pagans and Samaritans. Even a lot of Pharisees and Sadducees are annoyed with him over that."

I could feel, as he talked, that my mind could be with him but not my heart. So I responded, "Don't make a mistake. He says he has come for the sick and not for the healthy, and in political terms that means trying to make friends among those who, at the moment of the insurrection might be enemies. It is good preparation for the fight, don't you agree?"

He shook his head. "You've changed, Judas. Do you too believe that Jesus of Nazareth is the Anointed we were promised?"

I answered, "It might be that he is not, I can't bring myself to believe. But I know with no uncertainty that it is from the time of Moses that there has not appeared in Israel a man so capable of gathering a following among the masses. Whoever desires the liberation of our people today, must come to terms with him."

He pondered; perhaps he was tempted to agree with me. But then he replied, "Do you know how many visionaries there are now who are wandering around our land of visionaries? Do you have any idea how many demoniacs there are, and how many there are who, for better or worse, succeed in exorcising their demons? But I have never seen any of them get rid of a Roman. That's why Pontius Pilate allows them to live and multiply; they are innocuous, on the contrary, the more the people dream of the kingdom of heaven, the more they resign themselves to their subjection. We don't know what to do with Jesus of Nazareth. Do you know where he is?"

The question upset me; why in the world was he asking me? I replied, "I don't know. Maybe in Galilee. That's where we left him."

He looked at me with a mixture of scorn and compassion, and said, "He's here, in Jerusalem. If you want, I can also tell you in whose house he is staying. He's in hiding because he thinks the Jews want to kill him. In my view, the Jews have a lot more sensible things to do. Anyway, it could happen that he gets stoned. And it could be that some of his followers meet the same end. I don't understand what's the use of all this noise over some Galilean. Some say he's good, others that he's an impostor. He might be both things at the same time. I know that they're thinking about sending some guards out to get him."

50

So, he had come to Jerusalem without telling us a thing. John later explained that he hadn't said anything even to his brothers, on the contrary, he had deceived them as to his intentions, but, while he might have had something to fear from his brothers, what did he have to fear from us?

Anyway, he was in Jerusalem secretly, but not so secretly that the zealots didn't know it, and who knows how many others. He often acted that way. News of his presence had to travel covertly, remain uncertain, so that it created greater sense of expectation for his appearance. I was sure he would show up.

Indeed, with no warning, halfway through the feast, he appeared in the first courtyard of the Temple. We rushed over there as soon as we got the news. He saw us, certainly, but he didn't let on that he knew us, and we mixed in with the Judeans who were rushing in, without making ourselves evident but ready to come to his aid, if the need should present itself.

He waited until the crowd grew to a good size, then, calm and secure, even provocative, he asked the Judeans, "Why are you trying to kill me?"

Nobody answered. Most of them didn't even know who he was, they had simply followed the flow of people. He had a handsome face and an attractive presence, surely not violent despite the provocative attitude; why in the world would they want to kill him?

Then, having received no response, he began to teach: "I have not come on my own, but he who sent me, whom you do not know, is true. I come from him, and it is he who sent me."

His voice had a fascinating sound—he did everything he could to make it so—but his meaning, all things considered, was obscure, with the result that he enchanted some and irritated others.

Those who were enchanted said, "If the Anointed were to come, could he ever perform more miracles than this man has?"

The others, the ones who had escaped the enchantment, declared that he was nothing but another of the many imposters. Where were all these exalted miracles? He certainly hadn't performed any in Jerusalem, and as for those supposedly performed elsewhere, blessed be those who believe in them; stories told by women around the fire, on long winter nights, to leave their children with their mouths hanging open; miracles, if you want them, you've got to perform them yourself. So, the crowd was divided, some believed one thing and others believed the opposite, and there were heated discussions, things were on the verge of getting violent.

The authorities were not pleased by this kind of thing, and they were even less pleased by the exalted speeches of the prophet from Nazareth. Therefore, in agreement with the high priests, they sent the guards out to arrest him.

But he got away in time.

51

The last day, the most solemn day of the feast, he made another appearance at the Temple. He was very tense, he may have heard that there were guards out and about, sent to arrest him. He found a place in a corner of the courtyard and, standing on his feet, he began to shout: "Let anyone who is thirsty, come to me and drink. He that believes in me, as the scripture says, out of his belly shall flow rivers of living water."

As always, his obscure message divided the crowd. They inculcated in people blind acceptance or an equally extreme rejection, and among the Jews there were those who were saying that he was a prophet or even the Anointed, but most were of the opinion that he was a mad man, or one of the usual demoniacs who spewed out bizarre proclamations. But his voice, even if his words were incomprehensible, had a soothing sound, and his attitude, at least on that day, was meek. He might indeed be out of his head, but he was not dangerous.

So nobody dared touch him, even the guards sent to arrest him, who later got their fair share of reprimands from the doctors of law and Pharisees who were waiting inside the building. "Why haven't you brought him here?"

The guards replied, "No man has ever spoken like that."

Implicit in their response was the supposition that the Galilean to be arrested was something more than a man, and the doctors of law and Pharisees were irritated: "So you too have let yourselves be taken in by the gibberish of this Galilean vagabond? Look at us; is there perhaps one of us, doctor of law or Pharisee, who believes in him? Only imbeciles who know nothing of the Law let themselves be enchanted."

The guards, nevertheless, did not go back out to arrest him.

52

The next day at dawn, even though the feast was almost over, he was already back in the first courtyard of the Temple, and all of the people who arrived went over to crowd around him, and he spoke to them soothingly. As they listened, they grew more and more enchanted, and it seemed that it didn't really matter whether they understood him or not.

Later, some doctors of law and Pharisees came, presenting him a woman who had been caught in the act of adultery, and they asked him with feigned reverence, "Rabbi, you seem to know the Law better than we. Moses, in these cases, prescribes stoning; what do you say about it?"

Their question was designed to bait him because they knew that he always preached love and forgiveness. Now, if he replied that she should be forgiven, it would be easy to accuse him of violating the Law, while if he said she should be condemned, he would be in contradiction with himself.

The Rabbi appeared to be caught off guard, and in fact, instead of answering, he remained seated and started drawing in the dirt with his finger. The baiters, a bit irked but smelling their triumph, insisted on having a response, and that's when he raised up to them all the force of his conscience-penetrating gaze, and said calmly, "He among you who is without sin throw the first stone."

He said that and no more and went back to tracing in the dirt his incomprehensible signs, and the baiters, one by one, went away, leaving the woman to herself.

Then he stood up and approached her. "Nobody has condemned you?"

"Nobody, Lord."

"Nor do I condemn you. Go, and sin no more."

The people who had seen and heard crowded around him again, and nearly all of them had been won over.

53

Later on, those same doctors and Pharisees who had gone away in confusion, came back and approached him; surely, they had orders to gather testimony against him.

This time it was the Rabbi who baited them. Indeed, he interrupted the lesson he was giving on the beatitudes—he often spoke about them, with love and clarity—and staring into the eyes of his enemies, said in a firm and loud voice, so they would hear him well, "I am the light of the world."

It was a rather grand affirmation, and they couldn't let it pass without a response. They huddled together to consult and then one of them said, "You bear witness to yourself; that is not valid."

Calmly, with great solemnity, the Rabbi rebutted, "I am not alone, with me is my father who sent me. I bear witness to myself but my father who sent me also bears witness to me."

They consulted among themselves again, and asked, "Where is your father?"

The Rabbi made a gesture of annoyance and condemnation of their incapacity to raise themselves above the material and the contingent, and as though to challenge them he spoke even more enigmatically, "You do not know me or my father, if you knew me you would also know my father."

He went on still further in his obscure affirmations—even I did not understand the meaning of his words—and I wondered what in the world he was doing. Was he trying to remain obscure to avoid arrest—in fact, no one arrested him—or, on the contrary, was he trying to force things beyond the limits of tolerance? And in that case, was it only to test his own strength against theirs, or to see if he could accelerate the coming of his time that was taking too long to ripen?

No one knows.

Anyway, because nothing happened, an incurable melancholy descended upon him, and it was clear that he was having thoughts of death, but not without irritation for their failure to understand. He said, "I shall go, and you shall search for me. Where I go you cannot come. You are from down here. I am, and if you do not believe that I am, you shall die in your sins."

54

Having said that, as far as he was concerned the discussion was over, it was evident he wanted to leave. But his enemies, who had been ordered to compromise him, set themselves against him. "We do not accept such vague responses. You say, I am. What does that mean? Do you want to tell us clearly who you are?"

An indignant expression came over his face. I was expecting him to start shouting that he was the Anointed, the Messiah of the Messiahs, the son of the living God, and that he who did not believe in him did not even believe in the Eternal God of Israel, instead he stifled his fury, raised his eyes to heaven and replied, "When you will have lifted up the son of man then you shall know that I am, that I do nothing on my own, but I speak as my father has taught me. He who has sent me is with me, he never abandons me, because I always do what pleases him."

Even though what he said was not all that clear, his voice was soothing, and many were disposed to believe him. But he demanded more of those who wished to become his followers. He said, "If you abide in my word, you are truly my disciples, you shall know the truth and you shall be free."

It was a mistake. That expression—you shall be free—which in the Rabbi's intention was supposed to mean something else, disconcerted and irritated them; they were descendants of Abraham and they had never been slaves to anyone. They told him that in an unyielding tone.

He too became irritated, "I know that you are Abraham's seed, yet you are looking for a way to kill me because my word does not penetrate you. Just as I speak what I have seen at my father's side, so you do that which you have heard from your father."

In this way, he offended and humiliated them; what kind of surrender was he asking for? They were disposed to believe, but not to renounce the beliefs that they already had. "Our father is Abraham," they said.

He insisted, "If you were the sons of Abraham, you would do the works of Abraham. But now you seek to kill me, to kill the man who has told you the truth that he heard from God. This Abraham did not do. You do the works of your father."

The debate was turning into a fight. Someone in the crowd yelled out, menacingly, "We are not bastards; we have only one father, God!"

By now there was no way to make peace, nor even to offer him help, because instead of keeping quiet, he shouted out, infuriated, "You are of your father the devil! He that is of God hears God's words. You hear them not, because you are not of God."

They were more enraged than ever, and it was surely not the moment to try to explain to them that when he lost his patience, the Rabbi tended to use the word "devil" rather precipitously. They wouldn't have listened. They shouted in exasperation that he was possessed, a Samaritan, mad, a maniac, and so on, but as loud as they yelled, he in turn managed to shout over their voices, "Verily I say to you: before Abraham was, I am!"

Then those Judeans picked up rocks to stone him, and he was forced to run out of the Temple. It was easy because it was Saturday, and the streets were full of people coming and going.

55

The Judeans were tougher than the Galileans, and they could become dangerous if he insisted on provoking them. He must have realized on his own that it was better to take cover, and he was lucky because, making his way through the crowded streets, he saw a man—a beggar—who was blind since birth, and this so as to permit that the works of God should be manifested in him, and never had a manifestation presented itself so propitiously. He decided to perform a sensational prodigy.

He went over to the unfortunate wretch, conveniently attracted the attention of the passersby, then spit on the ground, used his saliva to make some mud, rubbed it on the eyelids of the blind man, and said to him, "Go and wash yourself in the Pool of Siloam."

The Pool of Siloam was always full of poor souls and curiosity seekers because, it was said, the sick who managed to jump into the water at the right moment came out healed, and so the fact that the blind man, after having washed himself at a moment that was not right, should come out seeing, did not go unobserved, and probably that was what the Rabbi had wanted to happen.

But when the man returned to his begging post shouting that he could see, things got complicated. Some, or rather many, claimed that the man who could now see was not the blind man from before, but another man, who looked like him. He could go on all he wanted that it was really him, they didn't believe him, and he explained that it had been a man named Jesus that had cured him, but he didn't know where Jesus could be found now.

It was on Saturday that Jesus had made the mud and opened the eyes of the blind man, and Saturday was a day of rest consecrated by our Eternal God. On the seventh day, it was prescribed: do not perform any work, not you or your son, nor your daughter, nor your servant nor your ox, nor your ass, nor any of your animals, nor your guest who stays within your doors, so that your servant and your maid shall rest as you do. The question was: was mixing mud and rubbing it on the eyes of a blind man to be considered work?

The answer was not easy, therefore they took the miraculously healed man and brought him to the Temple, to the doctors of law and the Pharisees.

However, in that circumstance, even the doctors and the Pharisees couldn't agree. The most agitated and intransigent said, "He worked on the Sabbath, therefore, he is a sinner."

"But" rebutted the moderates, "how can a sinner perform miracles?"

Well, perhaps Beelzebub had a hand in it, and anyway it was best to establish, first of all, if it really was a miracle. The miraculously healed blind man was there and they asked him, "What do you think of the man who opened your eyes? What do you say?"

And he, without any hesitation, said, "I think he is a prophet."

Then the doctors and the Pharisees had his parents brought in to testify that their son had been born blind, and they—poor souls fearful of the powerful—testified that yes, their son had been born blind, but as to the fact that it appeared that he could now see, they knew nothing: who can say, with certainty, if a man can see well or badly?

So the doctors and the Pharisees called in the miraculously cured man to have him explain yet again how things had gone—in brief, they wanted him to change his story—but since he insisted on saying again and again that he had been healed by Jesus of Nazareth, who certainly came from God—otherwise, how could he have opened the eyes of the blind?—they angrily expelled him from the sacred places as an imposter and spread the rumor that he was a false blind man who had conspired with a false prophet to deceive the people.

56

Outside the Temple, however, Jesus was waiting for him, and as soon as Jesus saw him he went over to him and said, "Do you believe in the son of God?"

The man replied, "Sir, who is the son of God that I should believe in him?"

And Jesus, "You see him; it is he who is speaking with you."

Then the miraculously cured man prostrated himself before him, saying, "Lord, I believe."

A few people had gathered to look on at what was happening, but all in all, that prodigy had not yielded as much as Jesus had intended. So, perhaps to remedy the situation, he launched into a parable in which he spoke of sheep and a shepherd, and of people who, instead of entering the sheepfold by the door, entered by climbing in through another opening, and certainly they were thieves or bandits.

Those who were listening found it difficult to understand what he was saying so he tried to explain, and things got even worse. He said in fact that he was the door, and that those who had come before him—that is, before there even existed a door, which, obviously, it wouldn't have been possible to use even if they wanted to—were thieves and bandits.

Now—the people asked themselves—who were those who had come before him? The prophets and kings of Israel? In this case, was it possible to refer to Abraham and Jacob, David and Samuel as thieves and bandits? Or was he not alluding to ancient kings and prophets but to the many improbable prophets who for some time now had been wandering between villages and the desert? If that's how it was, then he might be right, but what about the decapitated Baptist?

In sum, they were grumbling, and he, with the best of intentions to clarify things, said that he was not only the door to the sheep-fold, but also the good shepherd who gave his life for his sheep, something that, literally, also appeared to be incomprehensible, and in the end many of his listeners said, "He is possessed." And, "But why bother listening to him. He's delirious."

It was not a propitious day, and the Rabbi left.

57

The next day, he wasn't to be seen in the Temple, or in the city, and the same on the days that followed. We—Simon and I—thought that perhaps he had gone back to Galilee, or that he had withdrawn to the desert to pray, after that dubious mission in Jerusalem. We had no news of him, but the servant of a Pharisee, a man named Nicodemus—a good friend of the Rabbi—came to bring us some food and to tell us to wait.

We went to the Temple every day and stayed all day, talking about Jesus, so that the people would not forget him. We set ourselves against those who were convinced that he was possessed by a demon. Can a demon open the eyes of a blind man? In our view, he was the promised Anointed.

Many approved of what we said.

So then, when he returned to Jerusalem—it was winter, the feast of the Dedication, and one morning we found him walking in the Temple under the portico of Solomon—a small crowd gathered around him with sympathy and benevolence, saying to him, "How long are you going to keep us holding our breath? If you are the Anointed, say it openly."

But he did not like it when he was asked for guarantees and assurances, and he responded rudely, "I have already told you other times, but you do not believe. The works I do in my father's name bear witness to me. But you do not believe, because you are not my sheep. My sheep hear my voice, I know them, and they follow me; I give them eternal life and they will never perish, and no man will ever pluck them from my hand. My father who gave them to me is greater than all and no one will ever pluck them from the hand of my father. I and my father are one."

We were more than a little embarrassed, Simon and I. His discourse was garbled, and also rather harsh; they were not satisfied in the least. They had freely posed a direct question, and he replied—not without insolence—by losing himself in delusionary ramblings. It was already difficult enough for them to entertain the idea that this discontinuous and bad-tempered young man, a Galilean to boot, might be the Anointed, the culmination and resolution of a sacred history that had begun in Eden and had passed gloriously down through kings and prophets, and, instead of helping them and declaring openly, in a way that could then be discussed, "Behold, the Anointed and Messiah promised by God is here, I am he," he slipped into enigmatic expressions, which said and didn't say, eluded the real heart of the matter.

58

Indeed, what was to be understood from "I am" with no complement? And what meaning could be given to the phrase "My father and I are one," when, to the question "Where is your father?" he had responded with what amounted to a riddle? And then, why had he decided that they were not his sheep—they had no possibility of being so, from what could be understood—excluding them from eternal life and from other nebulous benefits and privileges?

They had every reason to feel that their good intentions were being flouted, so, together with others who had arrived in the meantime, they gathered up rocks with the intention of stoning him. They shouted out threats, and some who were more agitated than the others—but they might also have been emissaries of the doctors and Pharisees—started throwing them, without hitting him, however.

He showed no fear—his courage must have come more than anything else from the persuasion that his time had not yet come—and he apostrophized them calmly and shrewdly, even trying to make them feel guilty, "I have shown you many good works that come from my father, for which of those works do you wish to stone me?"

Even the most audacious kept their rocks in hand. One of them responded on behalf of them all, "We do not want to stone you for a good work, but because you blaspheme; you are a man and you make yourself equal to God."

It was a dangerous objection, and the Rabbi had to come up with the right answer if he did not want to put a premature end to his earthly life. He collected himself to meditate, then he spoke with prudence and cunning, citing the psalm of Asaf according to which all the children of Israel, being children of the Most High, are themselves gods. Why then did they accuse him of blasphemy if he said what was written in the Book, that which all Jews could legitimately say of themselves?

The argument was sacrosanct, and finally clear. Many among the Judeans let their rocks drop to the ground.

Then, inexplicably—maybe he felt too sure of himself, and forced the situation so that those who believed in him should overwhelm the others—he reassumed an arrogant tone, "I am sanctified by the father and by him sent into the world. How is it that you allow yourselves to say that I blaspheme if I say that I am the son of God, when even the Scriptures confirm that every man is such? If I didn't perform prodigies, you could not believe me, but I do perform them, and even if you do not want to believe me, you must believe in what I do. You must recognize then that the father is in me and I in him."

If it made any sense at all, this statement meant: all the sons of Israel are sons of God, but I am the son of God, with a special and privileged relationship for which I can perform prodigies, or better, I am all one with the father, with the Most High.

They could not accept either the statement or the tone with which he had pronounced it, and so the stones started flying again, many of them urged that he be captured, others tried to oppose them, it all turned into a huge chaos which he took advantage of to steal away.

It was an art that he knew well, and that he profited from, as long as he wanted to.

59

For yet a while more, we remained—Simon and I—without any news of him until the servant Nicodemus came to tell us that he was on the other side of the Jordan, in the places where John had baptized, and that we could join him. We decided to leave the next day.

That evening, at Aser's tavern, we met Ariel.

"The Galilean has power," he told us. "His gaze and his feats are majestic and authoritative. He is able, astute, brave, even brash. But he has no political sense. In a city already fragmented into a hundred splinter groups, he has brought new discord. We must unify, not divide, keep everyone together against Rome; even the doctors of law, the Pharisees, the Sadducees, as long as they are useful. We are glad that your Rabbi has gone away; we want him never to return. You two, what do you intend to do? We think you could stay in Jerusalem without running any risks. Those who were searching for you have forgotten about you."

I answered for both of us, "We're on our way to join him."

Ariel had a flash of anger, "But even you don't believe that he is the Anointed."

Simon said, "I believe."

Ariel turned to me, "But you don't, at least that is what you have led me to understand. You are educated, intelligent.

Try to examine your Rabbi with a little sense of the ridiculous; you'll find that he is little more than a charlatan."

I replied, "I belong to him."

His anger flashed again, more violently this time, "Just how much has he subjugated you, Judas? You used to be a solid man; at one time you were someone who could be counted on."

I replied, "I haven't changed, and I am more solid than ever; the liberation of Israel is my foremost thought. But I am certain that Jesus of Nazareth is the man best suited to bring us to the kingdom."

He realized that it was useless to insist, and said with heartfelt bitterness, "He'll end up being stoned or crucified. And not just him. Many of those who are tied to him will die too, and theirs will be useless deaths."

I was convinced of that as well, as far as I was concerned; however, it wasn't so much the uselessness as the necessity of my death that was involved, or rather, its inevitability. I bore its sign on my body, ever more evident. I said to him, "Ariel, I am getting to know the meaning of death, and I accept it. It may be that Jesus of Nazareth will not bring us to the kingdom, but I don't know what else to wait for. In these days I have seen Jerusalem: the Temple, the doctors, the Pharisees, the people how they act and think. I have seen that what happens is not just, and I no longer have the will to live."

He rebutted, after having reflected, "Do you think the others and I are happy about what can be seen in Jerusalem? Do you think that the others and I are not ready to die? But we would like to die for our nation, not because of weakness or desperation. Anyway, the two of you were part of our movement, and you have never betrayed us. If you have information that could be useful to the cause, be sure to let me know."

At dawn, Simon and I left Jerusalem and took the road that leads to the fords of the Jordan.

60

It was cold, the desert wind bent the dried-out shrubs thirsty for spring, we shivered in the only tunic that we had been granted.

The caravan trail went from one ridge to the other of yellow undulations, every so often we passed by camp sites where some caravan had stopped for the night, and now stray dogs were stubbornly searching among the meager refuse, rabidly contesting flesh-stripped bones, and we had nothing to give them, we carried no food with us, following instructions.

We walked without talking, Simon and I, he ahead and I behind; solitude was the condition to which You had accustomed and destined me, as is only right for him who must predispose himself for higher goals. I on Your right, no one on Your left, we two alone on the height of the throne to dominate nations, with splendor.

These were not fantasies to be cultivated; better to measure oneself against anxieties closer to home, to avoid ending up bitterly in disappointments and prostrations. In the last analysis, what had been put—or what I had put—in front of me was an unlimited but humble sacrifice, and when You spoke of thrones and recompenses and glories, my exclusion was understood, I was to find my only remuneration in what seemed to be the need that You had of me.

I felt proud of it, and vainly I asked myself if the sacrifice had been asked of me by You, and not instead offered to You by me. It wasn't easy to find the loose end in the knot of our communion and dependence. Even though it was indisputable, as a matter of fact, that I had come to offer myself, to beg You to take me, it was just as certain that by enchantment You had immediately roped me in at the first sight of You, and this was a font of hope and fear that You were truly the Anointed, the Coming from the Eternal, who for some obscure and mortal reason was in need of my death.

Anguished by doubts and uncertainties—in front of me the tenacious and obtuse stride of Simon whom uncertainties never touched—I prayed using ancient words, "Blessed art thou, our one Eternal God. Grant me intellect, incline my heart toward Your testimonies."

But where were the testimonies? In the cold air, in the dried-up shrubs, in the hunger of the dogs, in the fatigue of walking? In the thorn bushes that were not burning? Or was I to search for them within myself, in my disquietude and frustration, in my fervor that failed to find fulfillment, in my generosity and dedication that caught not a glimpse of recompense?

61

The answers wanting, I plunged into sadness. Remote the song of David: awake, psaltery and harp, I want to reawaken the dawn. When had I ever been close to the desire to reawaken the dawn with joy? My daybreaks had always been loaded with duties, abnegation, impatience, pride, will to power, boundless commitment to the Eternal of the armies, and for lack of anything better, the solicitude of death.

So that, Rabbi, when I came to You to tell You, take my life and try to make something of it for Yourself, I gave You a downright miserable gift. I was already consumed by questions, ready for the desert. Why such a frenzied craving for signs? Why so little peace in my heart? What's the use of suffering for nothing? Enjoy the pleasures of youth, Qoheleth admonished me. And I went off in a totally different direction.

In his land, our Eternal God allowed the wine that gave lightheadedness and forgetting, allowed foods pleasing to the palate, lilies to gather in the fields, herds to graze in the gardens, young girls with the inviting eyes of doves. How beautiful you are, my lovely, how beautiful! Your eyes are the eyes of a dove on the edge of a stream. And she replied: how handsome you are, my beau, how lovable, even our bed is verdant.

What overwhelming simplicity and delight, how vain the admonishment: enjoy life, my lad, because youth is a flash, blackness of hair a flash. O Qohéleth, the blackness of my hair would not come to an end, I bore a sign of election around my neck, and You, Jesus, knowing that, said, the hour is coming, and this is it. Good, I was ready to perform whatever task You should ask of me.

So, was it so ignoble to fantasize a place next to You on the throne of glory? Was I supposed to imagine perhaps that such a place belonged to John? Or to Peter? Who among us had given himself more deeply? Who would conduct himself with less dishonor when his hour arrived? The pain of my living, the anxiety to find its reason why, sealed off my heart. O temptation of the ridiculous! Simon and I, our tunics flapping, our feet sore, eyes red, sand on our lips, walking, stomachs gloriously empty, toward the liberation of our bastard people, the triumph of Israel, the end of time.

62

But, in You, I was unable to find the ridiculous, as much as I was aware of the extravagant aspects of Your adventures. Your days in Jerusalem had given me an image of You that was even more troubled and ambiguous. Never had I seen You so violent and fearful, rash and prudent, sad and provocative, contemptuous and submissive, mirror of the sacred city.

O Jerusalem encircled by hills, full of commotion, tumult, gaiety and shame, faith and ignominy! Three thousand Roman soldiers appeared to be sufficient to keep down a people that had also been chosen and blessed. Under the discrete protection of a pagan procurator, people carried on their trafficking and business activities without bothering to interrogate our Eternal God, nor did our Eternal God seem to be much on the minds of the doctors of law, Pharisees, and Sadducees and all the others who busied themselves in constructing a reasonable way of living in accordance with the Law and not in discord with Rome. This was the people You had gone looking for, Rabbi, and—desperate fracture and renunciation, delusion and bitterness—You had spoken to them with the vehemence of the ancient prophets: a people laden with iniquity, wicked race, the devil's offspring, you will never see glory!

But, if they were not destined for glory, how were we supposed to get there? Was not being Israel a common condition and commitment? Or, because of the people's iniquity, was the pact of alliance with the Eternal to be deemed broken, and You come to restore it, but excluding some and privileging others? O Lord, give me the intellect to understand, show me the way, I will follow it with all my heart.

I had placed my life in Your hands, and I was striving for it to become an act of faith, not of enchantment, but there was no help coming from You nor from him whom You called father. One time, in the Temple, when the exasperated Judeans started hurling stones at You, I found myself wishing they would kill You, in the end, even though I couldn't imagine what I would do with myself afterwards.

63

You were tough, Rabbi, much more so than You had promised. Tough not only with me—the absence of Your gaze if by chance our eyes met—but also with the Judeans, and not all of them wanted to imprison You or stone You, some of them wanted to believe in You, asked You for comfort in order to believe, and You wouldn't give it to them. They declared to You: we are enchanted by what You say, but we beg You, tell us who You are. And You gave them answers that were so obscure and entangled as to discourage them. There must have been some complicated reason for Your wanting to be misunderstood. With Your mad speeches, and Your brusque, irritating, imperious manner, You, Galilean, had gone to Jerusalem to propose Yourself beyond the limits of mystery, where no one could follow You without bewilderment, or absolute abnegation.

Did You go there to impose a risk, or to come to know one? When You provoked the Judeans in the Temple, was it in order to know their willingness to accept You without limits—an arduous condition of salvation—or their suitability to kill You? You were sure that Your time had not yet come—You drew more arrogance than confidence from that—but You wanted to know if, when Your time did come, they would be ready to do what had been written that they should do. But, suppose they had assumed the risk of accepting You without limits, what would they have gained from it? You would bring them the kingdom, You assured them, but in the meantime? I who had given myself without limitations still had disquietude and torments, and I was often tempted to think that this was due not only to my doubts, but also to Yours.

You would say, I am, and You proposed an infinity that had to be accepted in order to be. At the moment it was only possibility or hypothesis, a becoming that would not be realized without the involvement of everyone, without the confluence of everybody in an annulment that was the only possible glory, the end of time.

64

This You demanded—maybe there was no choice even for You—and my heart was frightened and my mind lost. This was not only about my death—I had pledged it to You immediately—but about the condemnation of the very principle of life, the creation of the father Adam turned out to have been a capricious error of the Most High, and perhaps the Most High had decreed that it was time the error was remedied. And You, to whom this extreme task had been assigned, more lost and frightened than us, spoke of love in order to give and receive relief. I, out of love—enchantment—had given myself, but not knowing the end, the waiting weighed on me. What had to be done was better done soon, if to that we were bound.

"If someone wants to follow me, he should deny himself, take up his cross and follow me." If someone wants to, You said, and You knew that it was fiction. To meet You was to follow You, or to be destined to the death and eternal damnation with which You threatened those who did not follow You. In their uncertain condition of responsibility for themselves, You charged mankind with an unbearable responsibility to live, indicating as the outcome a glory-death or a damnation-death, both immutable ends, eternal.

You would say to whomever You chose, "The son of man is about to come in the glory of his father with his angels: then he will deliver to each the retribution corresponding to his conduct." Did the corresponding retribution also involve the place at Your right hand or at Your left?

You created in us—Your twelve—an understandable rivalry, and also a legitimate impatience for the event, because we felt—they felt—worthy of the prize, the place. "I solemnly declare to you that some of those present will not die until they have seen the son of man come to reign."

Some, not all, and I was not in that number. Seeing the advent of the kingdom was not to be granted to me. For Your transfiguration, You chose Peter, James, and John; to them, in a vision, You displayed Your glory, and they saw it.

I had been chosen for another task, as yet not clarified, it was only understood that it involved an obligation of death.

65

On the other riverbank, in the same place where the Baptist had raised his preannouncing voice, hundreds and hundreds of people had gathered, and others continued to arrive from every part of Judea and Galilee, for the most part in groups, singing, praying, carrying the sick to be healed, demoniacs to be liberated, children to be blessed. Every now and again, here and there among the crowd, someone cried out in wonder, exultation, or thanksgiving; someone—perhaps someone who had nothing to do with us—had performed a prodigy in the name of Jesus of Nazareth. He did nothing to impede it. Those who are not against us, are with us, he had decided.

There was an air of triumph on the banks of the Jordan. Peter and Andrew, James and John, Philip and Bartholomew, Thomas and Matthew, James of Alpheus and Thaddeus had returned from their apostolic missions exultant and emboldened; they had announced to the people the advent of the kingdom, performed prodigies as they had been allowed to do, acquired large numbers of proselytes, and many had followed them just to see the Galilean whose disciples said was the promised Anointed, he who would liberate Israel from discord, sickness, need, the pain of living, and maybe even from the Romans, although this last did not seem to be of special concern to anybody.

It wasn't known just how so many people—they had come to number in the thousands, and most of them had left on the spot and empty-handed—could be fed, but somehow, they managed to eat, and even that came to be seen as prodigious. Indeed, such a vast throng must have been granted the protection of the Eternal, notwithstanding the impression that within the massive crowd there was more curiosity than faith, more extravagance than prayer, and besides, as always in similar circumstances, those seeking the Anointed out of hope or need were mixed together with thieves, informants, prostitutes, jugglers, peddlers, and, naturally, doctors of law and Pharisees, attentive to the respect of the law, ready to launch accusations, clever in spreading rumors, so that arguments and disagreements were not infrequent, as neither were imprecations and weeping for failed cures or unforeseen relapses into illness.

Nevertheless, the multitude, in its heterogeneous mass, had a spiritual grandeur about it, a fervor of expectation, an excited glee that continued to spread like a contagion the vague sensation that something that had been still had begun to move, that a bond had been formed between the sacred history that was taught in the synagogues and the history that was being made now with the participation of all.

Many people thought of Passover as a time of gathering, and Passover was not far off, near the river the bushes were not dry as they were in the hills, and the almond trees, already in bloom, were beginning to turn green. Passover, memory of a liberation, would bring—it was said—a new liberation, the Eternal would make his voice heard again; even now it could be invoked with confident good cheer. Four hundred years of silence were about to come to an end.

The last voice to sing had sung like this: "Behold, the day is coming, that shall burn as an oven, and all the proud, and all who behave impiously shall turn to stubble, and the day that is coming shall burn them up, and shall leave them neither root nor branch, but for you who fear my name the Sun of righteousness will arise and healing shall be in his wings, and you shall go forth and grow up as barn calves."

66

But he, the Rabbi, was sad; his incurable melancholy. Often, he was also distant in spirit, in some region where it was not consented to follow him. He performed healings, taught the disciples who gathered around him, prescribed prayers, told parables, sometimes inveighed against doctors and Pharisees who posed tricky questions in order to inculpate him; he did everything but with more diligence than ardor, as though the ardor of his spirit was by now absorbed by thoughts much beyond the reality that stood before him, as exultant though it might be.

He was no longer the Rabbi of before; in his covert and ambiguous journey to Jerusalem, in the tempest into which he had dragged his soul, in his silences and his dialogues with the father, he had matured a resolve that detached him from the earth, and from us.

Not from all of us, however. As soon as his commitment to the crowds allowed him a bit of rest, some time for himself, when he believed that day's toil to have been enough, then he went off on his own, we all around to defend his respite. If he was praying, he wanted to be alone, but when his meditation was not prayer, when his thoughts turned to leave taking and his presentiments led to sighs, then young

John was allowed to approach him, sit at his feet, rest his head on his knees, and share his sadness.

I was not jealous, never would I have dreamed of that kind of intimacy for myself; my spirit—darkly, doubtfully, tormentedly—still wished that he would order me to take up a sword against Rome, and I would have shown him what my arm was like. But the more we went ahead, the more I suspected that he would not make me die carrying a sword. He had other designs. He was a tough boss, as soon as he had the opportunity, he humiliated my unconditional passion.

When, having come to the fords of the Jordan, I presented myself to him to pay him homage—I had no prodigies to report, nor proselytes to exhibit—he held out the purse to me that I had given him when I left.

I said, "Rabbi, consent that the money be not mine but everyone's."

He replied, "It is everyone's. The purse contains not only what was yours, but also offerings gleaned by the others. You will keep the purse."

I would have liked to object that, for that particular task—keeping the common accounts—Matthew, who before had been a tax collector, was more qualified than I, but his mind was already elsewhere, no objections were allowed. Surely, it was John who had suggested to him to order me to keep the accounts, so he would later have a way to say—and he said it—that since I kept the purse, I was a thief. It is indeed true that, later on I had something to do with unclean money—the thirty pieces of silver—but without realizing it, by reason of mysterious obedience. I was one of those who had given everything on joining him, and even before that; he should have known. Yet that was not enough for him, he continually subjected me to new tests, perhaps to reassure himself that I would be up to the final test.

By now it was near, you could feel it in the air and in the people.

67

One day, knowing that the doctors and Pharisees were going around saying that he was casting out demons with the aid of the prince of demons, he got irritated: "If I cast out demons with the help of Beelzebub, with whose help do your disciples cast them out? But if instead I cast them out with the divine might of God, that means that the kingdom of God is crashing down upon you."

Those were his very words, that it was crashing down upon us—tremendous imminence—but he left to us—he always did—the responsibility to disentangle the premise: whether he cast out the demons with the power of the Most High, or of someone else.

In that climate of collective exultation, it seemed that everyone was more or less able to exorcise demons, and by virtue of whom or what they were able to do it was a rather controversial question, or futile, so that, to believe in him— in the Rabbi—not a few were asking for more signs.

Among the importuners, obviously, were doctors and Pharisees, who, at a certain point, said to him openly, "Rabbi, we want you to give us a sign."

His anger flared: "Unfaithful and adulterous race, why do you ask for a sign? No sign shall be given to you."

What was meant was that his presence, his appearance, his voice and his gaze, should have been signs sufficient to believe that he was. When all is said and done, he said, the announcement of Jonah had been enough for the people of Nineveh to change their lives. What was it, what sign were these people demanding now, given that they had before them someone who was much greater than Jonah?

He spoke above all to me, naturally, although usually I did not ask him directly for the sign, but the Eternal. By now, however, it appeared that there was no difference. There was no pity, nor understanding for my anguished questioning. Why do you remain so distant? Why do you conceal yourself in such difficult times?

He said: "No one lights a lamp to put it in a closet or under a bowl; it is put on a stand near the doorway so those who enter have light."

He was the light in the doorway, and I should have seen the light with the strength of my spirit. Instead, I was not able to give up the proud right to understand.

So, he sought me out with his gaze and fixed it on me: "Be careful lest the light within you be darkness."

It wasn't fair. I might have had little light within me, but who could say that there was not also darkness in him? What was it, beyond his power of enchantment, his cleverness in making the crippled walk, in giving sight to the blind and hearing to the deaf, in exorcising demons in abundance, what was it besides this that indicated him as the Anointed? You testify on your own behalf, the doctors of Jerusalem had reproached him. Why are you so averse to the risk of giving an unequivocal sign, of power or vanity?

No signs were given.

68

To the others too, when the occasion presented itself, you showed little mercy. "Deepen our faith," they would ask You, knowing that for You their faith was never enough, it was not faith enough to declare loud and clear that You were the Anointed, to believe that they would be with You in the kingdom. You demanded more. You used to say that if we had had a crumb of faith, no bigger than a mustard seed, we would have moved mountains, or transplanted mulberry trees in the middle of the sea.

Were we supposed to give the signs that You wouldn't? Move mountains, not merely traffic with demons, both dumb and speaking? Was it the absurdity of these proposals that caused Your incurable melancholy?

Sometimes, however, Your sad thoughts suffocated, You returned to the brashness of the early days, when You went to challenge Your own people in Your home town, and I loved You so much, then. You would say, "I have come to set the earth on fire, and how I wish the fire were already lighted."

I also loved You when You prayed, "Father, manifest the sanctity of your name, thy kingdom come."

But I loved You more when You talked about Your anguish and anxiety for the different kind of baptism that was waiting for You, because I knew that in Your new baptism of death I was both involved and necessary.

We were already on the road to Jerusalem.'

69

Naturally, the multitude—they came and went, were always new but in a certain sense always the same—didn't follow us; only the most convinced and available among them, and the women were numerous, because the Rabbi trusted and respected them, preached the things that enchanted them most—love and mercy—and did it suavely. They sang the wedding song for him: you are beautiful, more beautiful than all the sons of man, grace overflows from your lips, that is why God has blessed you eternally.

Now, on the road without a large crowd around us, we were more exposed to the schemes of our enemies. One day some Pharisees—maybe what they said wasn't true, they just wanted to make him worry—came running up to him to warn him: "Hurry up and leave this territory. Herod wants to have you killed."

He was totally unimpressed; what he was destined to face was certainly not a death at the hands of Herod. In his departure from this world there were much different aspirations and complications, and maybe even scriptures, to be observed. So, he responded, "Go tell that fox that I am still here casting out demons and performing cures today and tomorrow, and the next day I will take up my journey again because it cannot be that a prophet should perish outside of Jerusalem."

His answer, begun with insolence, had ended in sadness. Then he added in a whisper, "Jerusalem, Jerusalem, you who kill the prophets and stone to death those who are sent to you by God."

This, then, was the significance of his hidden and solitary visits to Jerusalem; to assure himself that it was there that they killed the prophets and the messengers of God.

He called us off to the side, we twelve, and said to us, "Behold, we are going up to Jerusalem, and everything that was written by the prophets about the son of man will be accomplished. He will be delivered up to the pagans who will scorn him, insult him, spit on him, and, after having flagellated him, they will kill him. But on the third day he will rise again."

They, the other eleven, the ones he had called, those who never missed a chance to proclaim him the Anointed, the Promised, the Coming, perhaps too caught up in fighting over places of prominence next to the throne of the future kingdom, understood nothing of what he had said; it all remained a mystery to them, and they did not perceive its significance.

I, my heart tight, exulted; this was the beginning of the revelation: the connection between fantasy and reality, between the obscure talk and history. There was no doubt that the pagans who would offend, torment, and kill him, must be the foreigners who occupied our land. How could the others fail to understand?

Disappointed by their incomprehension, the Rabbi shut himself even more inside his melancholy, but his gaze could not help but seek me out.

And my eyes, adoringly, answered him, "Fear not, Rabbi. I will be."

70

The hour is coming, and this is it; by now they were all saying it.

My impatience came to the fore again; Eternal God, hasten to answer me.

Secret signs were running through the crowd; they were perceptible. From the breast of dawn, the youth of Israel was going to him like the dew. High atop the mountain, perfect in its beauty albeit deprived of its sanctity, Jerusalem waited.

When I cry out, answer me, God of my justice.

No response to so much anxiety for accomplishment; his moving toward divinity, triumph, glory, self-destruction, or whatever else he had in mind, was quite slow, hindered by small incidents and nuisances.

It cannot be that a prophet should perish outside of Jerusalem, he had said with magnificence, but he delayed by engaging in futile discussions, by performing the most banal prodigies that added nothing to his fame and grandeur. At this point, what could be the value of curing yet another blind man, or adding another demon to the number of those already cast out?

One day we were going through the city of Jericho, on the road to Jerusalem, a large crowd looking on, and a man, small in stature, unable to get a view of the Rabbi from behind the line of people, had climbed a sycamore tree and was perched on a branch. The Rabbi, passing nearby, looked up and saw him, and even though he had presumably never seen him before—so many things are unexplained—spoke to him, calling him by name, "Zacchaeus, come down from there, because tonight I want to stay at your house."

Evening drawing near, it was understandable that he should look for shelter for the night, a house that was hospitable and safe.

But this Zacchaeus, oddly perched on the sycamore—a nice manifestation of curiosity, if not faith—was very rich and, like nearly all rich people, more than a little disreputable. In fact, he performed the functions of the head collector of customs duties, so practically speaking, he took money from the Jews and gave it to the Romans, keeping for himself, obviously, more than a small part of it; an occupation that the Rabbi, according to what he had been preaching all this time, should not have appreciated much.

Nevertheless, he had practically invited himself, it is fair to say, to stay at his house, and on seeing this, everybody, not only the doctors and the Pharisees, started murmuring resentfully that the Galilean, who was so fond of proclaiming his holiness, had gone to stay in the house of a reprobate.

There wasn't much to be said against this allegation; that man was a reprobate. But it is not impossible that an impious man, in propitious circumstances, should become pious, and this is precisely what happened when the rich man Zacchaeus stood up and solemnly announced that he would give half of his wealth to the poor, and that he would restore to the victims of his extortions four times what he had stolen. Imagine how much he had stolen.

71

Other times, Rabbi, You wouldn't settle for half measures. The condition for being one of Your followers and winning a place in the kingdom was giving all of what one had, even one's life.

How is it that, for that Zacchaeus, who said he would give only half, You exalted? Indeed, full of joy on hearing him, You proclaimed: "Today, this house has known salvation, because he too is the son of Abraham, and the son of man has come to look for and save what had been lost."

Those were not the most just words to pronounce before an audience that was already complaining; they were expecting to see the appearance from one minute to the next of the kingdom of God—and behold, You, who that kingdom had announced and asserted, You gave Yourself to singing the praises of one who, up to the minute before, had persecuted the poor and humble.

You Yourself must have noticed Your error and their hostility, and perhaps with the intention of rectifying the situation, You set about reciting a parable; unfortunately, it was the most abstruse and least merciful of Your parables. To be sure, while listening it was necessary to go beyond the literal meaning to understand the secret meaning, but it wasn't so easy to do. You were talking about money, profits, bank accounts; in the home of Zacchaeus.

How challenging Your words, how much one needed to love You not to lose heart.

72

This is the story the Rabbi told in the home of Zacchaeus.

A nobleman who was going to a distant town to be crowned king had entrusted his servants with a sum of money, ordering them to traffic until his return. His fellow countrymen, who hated him, sent a delegation on his heels to tell him they did not want him as king. When he returned with the investiture of the kingdom, he sent for those servants to whom he had entrusted the money, to find out how much each of them had earned from their trafficking.

The first servant presented himself and said: "My Lord, your money has yielded ten times as much," and the king, satisfied, entrusted to him the government of ten cities.

Then a second one came, saying, "Your money, My Lord, has earned five times as much," and he was given the government of five cities.

Then another one came and said, "My Lord, behold your money which I have kept here in this handkerchief because I was frightened of you because you are a tough man. You take what you have not put up and reap what you have not sewn."

And the king said to him: "I will judge you by your words, wicked servant. You knew that I am a tough man, who takes what I have not put up and reaps what I have not sown. Why did you not at least deposit the money in a bank, and on my return, I would have withdrawn it with interest?"

Then, addressed to those present: "Take that money from him and give it to the first servant."

They all objected: "But My Lord, he has already had ten times as much."

And the king: "I say unto you that to whomever has will be given, but from whomever has not will be taken even what he has. And as for my enemies, who did not want me to reign over them, conduct them here and cut their throats in my presence."

73

Rabbi, Jesus, I know that though You spoke of money we were to understand something else—the gifts that the Eternal had granted us—and I know it is a sin of omission and neglect not to use for the good of mankind and the glory of God the gifts that the Eternal has granted. But I—I who had only what I had given You—I, listening to You, was led to identify with the third servant, the one who, not having any business sense, had kept the money in a handkerchief.

And You, with whom did You identify?

You, on the first night of our binding sodality—the two of us were alone, beneath the stars, stretched out in our mantles and a stone for a pillow waiting for sleep—You had told me that You were a tough man, that You took what You had not put up and reaped what You had not sown.

Was it You, Lord, the king who demanded that his enemies have their throats cut in his presence?

To be sure, Israel also needed men who were ferocious if it wanted to liberate herself from Rome. Ariel and the other zealots from Jerusalem were ferocious. But You, didn't You indicate another way for us? Where were Your words of love, Your exhortations to forgiveness? Where were the enticements: knock and it will be opened unto you, ask and it will be given to you?

Pure propaganda?

74

Luke wrote that, having left the home of Zacchaeus, You started out on the climb toward Jerusalem, where You entered the city riding on a donkey colt.

John, however, tells another story, full of adventure, turn-abouts, dramatic surprises, ingenuity and cunning, splendor and misery. A story that was finally supposed to be the sign—awaited and demanded—of Your divinity: a resurrection from death.

Now, we knew that in faraway lands, to the East, there were rabbis who succeeded in remaining suspended in the air, and in entering into death, shutting themselves into graves without water and food, to then return to the light. You Yourself had succeeded in walking on the waters of the lake, as some of Your followers testified, and You had performed, on the daughter of the head of a synagogue, an uncertain resurrection; maybe she was sleeping as You Yourself said.

But the resurrection of Lazarus of Bethany was different, public, and clamorous, done in defiance of those—perhaps all of us—who still did not believe enough.

We were, then, still outside of Judea, in one of the many small villages, whose name has been forgotten, when they came to advise You that Lazarus—whom You loved—the brother of Martha and Mary—whom You loved—was sick.

You showed no surprise, nor worry. "This illness is not fatal, but it is the glory of God, so that the Son of God will be glorified."

An opportunity, therefore, to demonstrate the power of the Eternal—and Yours—like the man born blind in Jerusalem. But this time there were to be no doubts—is it him or not, was he born blind or not—so it was necessary that the prodigy happen unequivocally, in front of many unimpeachable witnesses.

Despite the gravity of the news, we stayed two more days in the village where we were, then You said: "Let us go to Judea."

Your intimates must have been informed by You about Your secret trips to Jerusalem—and perhaps You had exaggerated the risks You faced—so when they heard Your proposal they said in alarm: "Rabbi, the Judeans have just tried to stone you, and you want to go back there?"

You responded: "Aren't there twelve hours in a day? Those who walk in daylight do not stumble because they see the light of this world, but those who walk at night stumble, because they have no light within."

We were used to Your obscure talk, we accepted it for what it was, no questions asked. But later I tormented myself with self-interrogation. Did You want to say that there would be no danger for You, because You would walk only by day, perhaps moving with the caution of a serpent? Or rather that You were the light of this world and they—who masked their fear with apprehension for You—would not run any risk by following You to Judea? But: who was going to stumble because he had no light within? One day You had said "Be careful that the light within you does not go dark," and I felt those words on my body, spoken especially for me, since I was reluctant to proclaim in a loud voice and in every moment that You were the Anointed. The signs You gave were insufficient, and I would not renounce the right to criticize You; I was not a servant.

75

As a free man, I saw the error You had made in the home of Zacchaeus, and I foresaw the one You would commit by going to Lazarus. Was it not perhaps a step backward, on the path to glory, to go to the aid of a friend, who by the way was not lacking the money for doctors and medicine? And precisely at this point a resurrection so that the works of God would be revealed? Hadn't You already performed enough prodigies?

When I cry out answer me, my merciful God.

You said: "Our friend Lazarus has fallen asleep, but I will go to wake him."

They didn't understand, and they didn't even want to understand: Bethany, the village where Lazarus had so inopportunely fallen asleep, was right outside the gates of Jerusalem, where it was possible to run into doctors of law, Pharisees, temple guards, and who knows maybe even Roman soldiers, ready to capture the prophet with all of his followers. So they said to themselves: but what is the matter if he has fallen asleep? Why the need to wake him?

Then You said openly: "Lazarus is dead, and I am happy for you not to have been there, so that you will believe."

Good Heavens, but if they did nothing else but say unto You that You were the Anointed, the Coming, the Awaited, the Savior, what else did they have to believe?

"Let us go to him," You said.

Despite everything, there was a moment of doubt, of indecision, until Thomas, turning to us, said: "Let us also go to die with him!"

They set off with resolve, and I behind them. The advice of Ariel came to mind, to look at things with a bit of the sense of the ridiculous. Simon, I knew, carried a dagger with him, hidden under his tunic. But Peter displayed, with unpredictable nonchalance, a sword he had picked up who knows where. Bind your sword to your side, brave man, dress yourself with the glory of your magnificence!

We arrived without incident, at the first houses of Bethany, and we stopped there, to find out a little more.

76

Since Bethany was just over two miles from Jerusalem and was almost a suburb of it, many Judeans from the capital had gone to visit Martha and Mary to console them for the death of their brother; their house was full of people. When Martha learned—a boy sent by us informed her separately—that the Rabbi was about to arrive, she dropped everything and ran to meet him. Mary remained seated in the house and talking with their guests.

Martha reached us out of breath and threw herself at the feet of Jesus, saying to him: "Lord, if you had been here my brother would not have died. But I know that now, whatever you should ask of God, he will grant it to you."

We understood, with emotion, that she was asking for an exceptional prodigy—a resurrection from the dead—and he too understood that she was asking him for it. Indeed, he answered her, "your brother will rise again."

And Martha: "Yes, I know he will rise again; in the resurrection on the last day."

Hers was a surprising response; it could have even seemed more ironic than bitter, after she had made him promise the prodigy. I feared he would explode in anger.

But he didn't explode, on the contrary, he said to her calmly: "I am the resurrection and the life. He who believes in me, even if he dies, will live, and whoever lives and believes in me will never die. Is this what you believe?"

The Rabbi's response was also surprising; there he was talking about eschatology while there was a dead man lying there, who, as was specified shortly thereafter, stank. Anyway, Martha answered dutifully: "Yes, Lord, I believe that you are the Anointed, the son of God, who was to come into the world."

Having pronounced solemnly this affirmation of faith, she took her leave. We stayed, I full of suspicions: too much ambiguity.

77

Martha arrived back home, went over to her sister, and whispered to her, "The Rabbi is here and he is calling for you."

Mary stood up trembling with emotion and went outside, and the Judeans who were there to comfort her, thinking that she was going out to weep in front of the sepulcher, didn't want to leave her alone and promptly ran after her.

It was thus that the encounter of Mary, sister of Lazarus, with Jesus of Nazareth, and the subsequent resurrection performed by him, had several, important, and unimpeachable witnesses.

Throwing herself at his feet, Mary said to him, "Lord, if you had been here, my brother would not have died."

Seeing her weep, and with her the Judeans who accompanied her, he was shaken by a tremor and became upset. Then he asked, "Where did you bury him?"

They answered him, "Lord, come and see."

He was crying, and the Judeans said, "Look how much he loved him."

But others commented, "He opened the eyes of the blind man, couldn't he have done something to keep him from dying?"

They were not hostile to him, on the contrary, in one way and another they expressed wonder, curiosity, and expectation.

We came to the sepulcher, a cave whose entrance was blocked by a rock. Shaken again by a tremor, the Rabbi said, "Roll back the rock."

It was then that Martha, having arrived together with some others, pointed out to him that they had buried him four days ago, and so his body surely stank.

He looked at her, with disapproval, and said to her, "Haven't I told you that if you believe you will see the glory of God?"

So, they rolled back the rock, and he, his gaze turned to heaven, his face resplendent with majesty, in a loud voice, so that everyone could hear him clearly, said, "Father, I thank you that you have heard me. I knew well that you always hear me, but I am speaking for the people around me, so they will believe that you have sent me."

Then, turning his gaze to the open grotto, with an imperious voice, he shouted, "Lazarus, come forth!"

The dead man, hands and feet bound by wrappings and his face wrapped in a shroud, came out.

He said, "Unbind him and let him go."

78

This then was the sign granted to those who did not believe so that they should believe: a wondrous sign, solemn, public, indubitable.

Rabbi, Jesus, Your other prodigies I might even have believed—You possessed extraordinary metapsychic powers—but the resurrection of Lazarus was a calculated, cool-headed, orchestrated fraud.

Every detail had been studied to get the desired effect: nothing was left to chance. The news of the death brought to us in the distant village—but You knew that Lazarus was already thought to be dead—the backing and forthing before deciding to enter Judea, Your elusive word play between sleep and death, and finally the news and the decision: he is dead and let us go to him and you will be forced to believe after you have seen what I am going to do.

Many others, apart from us, would be forced to believe.

Bethany was not Jerusalem, but the echo of what was happening there easily reached the capital. The house of the deceased to be resuscitated—he was a prominent figure in the village, wealthy, and connected to the Jerusalem bourgeoisie—would be full of people, and You had purposely waited two days before moving, so that news of the death would spread, and the Judeans would have time to get there.

We had approached the village cautiously; it was not a time for taking risks, it was wiser to have reliable information, and on the other hand the entrance had to be arranged just right. You sent ahead to call the two sisters, one at a time, each of them had a task to perform. The first informed You of the situation, testified—with that disconcerting comment about the resurrection on the last day—that her brother was quite dead, proclaimed that You were the Anointed son of God. The second brought You a trail of well-disposed Judeans. Then, calculating every gesture, expression, word— oh, that reasoned invocation of the Father!—You called Lazarus to come forth.

I couldn't avoid seeing the whole event with a sense of the ridiculous, and my temptation to believe You were the Anointed vanished. The sign You had given—or that the Eternal had given by Your means—was undoubtedly vain. But while—with pain and regret if I thought of my solitary dreams of our early days—I lost the hope of faith, I acquired a certainty: You were, in Your own way, a soldier of fortune. Certainly, not the splendid king, who with vassals and fanfare, on his sumptuous chariot of war, moves against the enemies of God and of Israel, but You were nevertheless a leader, You knew how to inspire the crowds, and how to insinuate Yourself among the ranks of Your enemies to then attack them from behind. With those inexplicable journeys to Jerusalem You had gained experience, and now You were gathering the fruits, separating those who were not with You but neither against You—and so recuperable—from those—the high priests, the authorities of the Sanhedrin— who would be against You in any case, and whom it was advisable to exasperate, to induce them into losing their judgment, to reduce them to a minority without a following, disdained by the bourgeoisie as well as by the people.

Unexpectedly, at just the right time, You got Your political wits about You: before moving on Jerusalem, it was better that the city should be within Your grasp.

79

Many of the Judeans who had gone to Martha and Mary's and had seen with their own eyes what Jesus had done, believed in him. But some—only some—went to the Pharisees to report.

The Pharisees and the head priests convened the Sanhedrin. "What shall we do?" they said. "This man is performing a lot of prodigies. If we let him go on like this everyone will believe in him and the Romans will come to destroy the Temple and the nation."

They didn't know which side to take.

But one of them, Caiaphas, who was the high priest that year, said, "You don't understand anything at all, and you don't realize that it's better to send one man to death for the people rather than let the whole nation go to ruin."

It wasn't clear what he meant by for the people, anyway from that day on they decided to send Jesus to his death, and they gave the order that anyone who knew where he was should denounce him so they could arrest him.

The Rabbi found out about this and was irritated by it. He wasn't expecting such a drastic resolution from the Sanhedrin. It was wise to let them have some time to think about it, and so the Judeans who had just been won over by the resurrection of Lazarus could make themselves heard.

To be on the safe side we left Bethany and withdrew to an area close to the desert, in the city called Ephraim.

By now, Passover was approaching, and a lot of Judeans were going up to Jerusalem to purify themselves before the feast, and they looked for Jesus of Nazareth in the city and in the Temple, and asked one another, "What do you think? Will he come to the feast?"

Auspiciously, the expectation of his appearance was growing. If the prophets could not do without Jerusalem, neither could Jerusalem, or so it seemed, do without the prophets, and Jesus of Nazareth, who was teaching new things and performing never-seen prodigies, was the greatest and most powerful prophet to be found in those times in the land of Israel.

The Rabbi was informed daily about these things that were happening in Jerusalem. It wasn't possible not to go there. Passover was only six days away. We set off on our way and stopped in Bethany, at the house of Lazarus.

The place was still enveloped in the atmosphere of the miracle, and there was a continuous flow of Judeans who came to confirm that he had really been resuscitated, and he obviously showed himself to be alive and happy to be so, and proclaimed that it had been Jesus of Nazareth who had summoned him out of his grave; and what other sign were they still waiting for to believe that Jesus was the Anointed, the promised Son of God?

They believed, and everything said it was also time to march on Jerusalem.

80

There, in the house of Lazarus, on the very evening of the stopover, an unpleasant incident occurred, with a woman, a bottle of perfume, and a lot of indignation.

All of Your biographers, Rabbi, talk about the incident, but some of them have it happen earlier and others later, some in one house and some in another, according to some the perfume was poured on Your head and according to others on Your feet, one says that the prodigal woman was a known sinner, but the others don't say that. All of them, however, agree that, in various ways, the episode stirred up scandal.

Matthew says that it was the disciples who were scandalized; all of them it seems. But according to Mark only some of them, unspecified, were indignant and said, "Why this waste of perfume? It could have been sold for three hundred dinars, that could then have been given to the poor." According to Luke, the indignant one is an ordinary Pharisee, to whose house You had gone for lunch.

And John?

John recounts that they had prepared dinner for You that evening at the home of Lazarus, the resuscitated being among Your dinner companions, with Martha serving at table. And then, suddenly, Mary, the fervid one, took a libra of authentic perfumed nard oil, quite precious, and poured it over Your feet, which she then dried with her hair. The perfume spread throughout the house.

Then, says John, Judas Iscariot, one of Your disciples, the one who was about to betray You, said, "Why wasn't this ointment sold for three hundred dinars for the benefit of the poor?"

And, John explains, I had said this not because I had the poor at heart but because I was a thief and, taking advantage of my having been entrusted with the purse, I took everything that everyone put in it.

You know, Jesus, that that's not true. I was born to a rich father, and I had turned my back on riches even before I met You. Money had no value for me, and therefore it could well be that the accounts were not always in order; I gave to anyone who asked me, without recording it.

Then, when it came time to betray You, they put thirty coins of silver in my hand, one-tenth of the value of that libra of ointment. Tell me: could I have betrayed You for money, receiving so little in return? There must have been an intention, a significance to that number, a prophecy; so, I took what they gave me.

John did not love me—nor I him—and whenever he had the opportunity, he defamed me. Nevertheless, when he later wrote Your story, he was the only one who told the truth with regard to my betrayal, and not even in a very concealed way. But, at the time he was writing, many years had gone by since the day on which I hanged myself from a tree, and by that time I had become, in the idea of the world, the traitor. The one who had delivered You up to Your enemies to be put to death, and nothing, not even the true story, could modify that judgment.

The next morning, the hour finally having come, we started on our way.

High atop the mountain, perfect in its beauty, Jerusalem awaited its liberator.

81

Exult wholeheartedly, O Daughter of Zion, send out cries of joy, O Daughter of Jerusalem. Behold: your king comes to you. He is just and victorious, humble, and mounted on a donkey, on the colt of a donkey.

Words of the Eternal on the lips of Zacharias, and they were to be observed.

The Rabbi called two of his disciples and sent them ahead to the village, "As soon as you enter there you will find a tethered donkey colt that has not been mounted by anyone; untie him and bring him to me."

The two went off and came back with the donkey. We threw our mantles over his back and the Rabbi climbed on top.

The enterprise began in a rather understated manner, but it had the comfort of ancient promises. I sent a boy whom I could trust to advise Ariel that we were marching on Jerusalem.

On the lips of Zacharias, the Eternal continued: I will make the wagons of Ephraim disappear; the horses of Jerusalem, the bows of war will be annihilated. Whatever the meaning of those words, this was the hour.

To be sure, notwithstanding Peter's sword, we were not a column of warriors, but we were people, animated by hope, faith, or anyway a desire to change, and we had a leader of great spiritual power, who in three years of public mission had won over innumerable followers.

Even now, as we walked along, our number was growing rapidly. Many of the Judeans who had gone to visit Lazarus, having learned of our departure, were joining us, and the groups and caravans who for their own reasons were going up to the feast joined us too, without knowing what our intentions were—actually, we didn't even know ourselves. It seemed that we were on our way to the conquest of a kingdom, and anyway there would be a revolution in accordance with the scripture—but it was enough for them to know that the man riding toward Jerusalem on a donkey was Jesus of Nazareth, the prophet who was being talked about throughout the land of Israel, the one whose commands were bowed to by demons, sickness, even death itself.

The crowd began to shout hosannas, play the pipes, beat their hands and drums. In short, the group that surrounded and accompanied the Rabbi turned into a crowd, where everybody was shouting wildly, acclaiming, imploring, pushing, and shoving. The most impassioned stretched out their mantles or palm leaves or olive branches before the donkey, as in the path of kings. And indeed the Rabbi's face shone with regal majesty.

82

But his face had neither a smile nor delight. Those who knew him—I looked at him with anxiety—understood that his spirit was uneasy. Was he frightened of the difficulties and the dangers that could lie ahead, or was it his incurable melancholy that was re-emerging even in this hour that had been promised triumphant?

Now, people were coming to join us even from the city of Jerusalem, numerous and festive. Among them were pilgrims who had already arrived in the city for Passover, Judeans who had been present when he had called Lazarus forth from the sepulcher, and others who had heard from family and friends the account of that prodigy, and finally a multitude that came running because they saw others come running, and were asking, "Who is he? What's happening?"

The answer was, "He is the prophet Jesus of Nazareth in Galilee." Then they too started shouting what they heard the others shouting, "Blessed is he who comes in the name of the Lord! Hosanna in the highest!"

The sad young man sitting on the donkey was engulfed in a festive commotion, the inebriation of victory. Rising up on the horizon, in all its beauty, the joy of all the earth, was Mount Zion. Beautiful was the city of the great king, and a king even greater than David was riding up to her to liberate her from her temporary servitude.

When we were near the city gate—not a shadow of danger to be seen—Peter put himself in front of the donkey to lead the way, and shaking his sword he shouted, "Hail the Son of David!"

We disciples and followers, and everyone who could hear us—men, women, and especially children—repeated ardently, "Hail the Son of David!"

The people recognized in him the promised Anointed, the Awaited, the Savior.

A Pharisee—there were a lot of them there in the crowd—managed to get up close to the Rabbi and shouted, "Don't you hear what they're saying? Tell them to be quiet!"

The Rabbi shook himself out of his melancholy and answered fiercely, "If they were to fall silent, the stones would begin to shout that I am the Son of David!"

Then he quickly grew sad again, and started weeping over Jerusalem, with words that only a few could hear because of the applause, the acclamations, the invocations, and benedictions.

The Pharisees were beside themselves, accusing one another, "Don't you see that you've accomplished nothing, they have all become his followers."

In effect, they were all behind him, having already entered the city of Jerusalem, in a triumphal procession down the street that leads to the Temple. Louder and louder, the crowd kept on shouting his name, and said, "He is the Anointed! He is the king! The king of Israel! Hosanna!"

This was the hour that had been dreamed about and so long awaited, and now it all seemed to be going too easily, with no opposition, there would be no combat. The soldiers of Rome, by order of the procurator Pontius Pilate, had withdrawn inside the Tower of Antonia. What was happening in Jerusalem was certainly not an armed uprising—Peter's sword was covered with rust—and if a new prophet from the provinces—they had seen plenty of others—wanted to go up to the Temple, let the Sanhedrin take care of it. They had their guards, let them do something if they should find it opportune,

But the Sanhedrin didn't know what orders to give, beyond the one already given, ineffective, to arrest him. The guards wouldn't have obeyed, even at the Feast of the Tabernacles they had shown their fear and their subjection to him.

By now it was clear: we would be able to reach the Temple and take possession of it without any problem. And then? Who would drive the Romans out of the Tower of Antonia? What were the zealots up to? They had weapons and they were combat trained; why didn't they take advantage of all this confusion, of the size and the exultation of the crowd, to attack the Tower and the palace of the procurator?

"I'm going to find Ariel," I said to Simon, and I let them go on their way.

83

It was a struggle getting into Aser's tavern; the door opened onto the street leading to the Temple, and all the patrons—pilgrims, artisans, shopkeepers, prostitutes—were gathered around outside to watch the crowd, which, like a tumultuous torrent, was following the new prophet, or king or whatever, and they too were shouting at the top of their voices, "Hosanna to the Son of David! Hosanna to the King of Israel!"

They barely let me pass, pummeling me with questions. You were at his side, why have you come away? Is it true that he resuscitates the dead? Does he really forgive adulterers?

A beggar, who pulled himself along the ground since he had been born without legs, was in desperation because no one would help him up. They wouldn't let him see the prophet who brought the dead back to life. He was convinced that, if he could manage to see him, he would have grown legs. When he learned that I was one of the disciples, he grabbed on to my tunic, imploring me to try to get them to grow. I pushed him aside, not without annoyance: a prodigy like that was beyond even the Rabbi's powers.

Ariel, together with two other leaders whose names were Mahat and Emon—they were the triumvirate at the head of the insurrection movement—were sitting at a table, a pitcher and glasses in front of them, and they were talking quietly among themselves, showing no emotion, as though there weren't a pandemonium in progress the likes of which had never been seen in Jerusalem, and as though it wasn't very important that Jesus of Nazareth, a man who had come forth from the people of Israel, a true prophet, perhaps the Anointed, the liberator king promised for centuries, was taking possession of the city. And these were the best sons of Jerusalem?

I couldn't hold back my disdain. "What are you waiting for to give the order to start the insurrection? I thought this city was full of spirited youth, impatient to take up arms. Now a harmless Galilean, sustained by the force of his spirit and by the favor of an entire people, is occupying the city and the Temple, and what are you doing? Are you still carrying on your revolution of words? Can't you hear the shouting, the hosannas? They're acclaiming him king."

Ariel nodded me to take a seat and poured me a drink. The one whose name was Mahat said matter-of-factly: "We've seen other prophets and other insurrections in Jerusalem. Even taken part in some of them. More than a few of us have ended up hanging from a cross. You know that. You too have taken risks. What has been the result of these uprisings, born of sentiment? The dominion of Rome has become more efficient and harsher. The procurator is in Jerusalem now, precisely because during the feast it's more likely that an uprising will break out, and he wants to keep the city under control. The tetrarch Herod is here too, he arrived yesterday. Evidently, they too were expecting Jesus of Nazareth. If they let him get as far as the Temple, then they don't fear him. A century of legionnaires would have been enough to keep him from entering the city."

My indignation raged because these revolutionaries had no faith in the people. They believed only in the organization, in the structure. And they were also in bad faith. Since the movement of the Galileans hadn't been founded by them and was not under their control—the king on the throne would be Jesus of Nazareth, not Mahat, much less Ariel or Emon—they didn't support him; on the contrary, they were trying to diminish him, to ridicule him. I said, "Not one, but not even ten centuries would have been able to stop us. You don't appreciate the strength that Jesus draws from the crowd. A lot of them would be ready to die, if he asked them to."

Mahat responded again, "I don't doubt it, but it's better to die for something useful. What has your Rabbi accomplished? What is his political philosophy? His enemies seem to be the Pharisees, the doctors of law, the priests. None of that is very interesting to us, even worse, we think that it's bad for the cause to create more discord, beyond that which already divides us. This Galilean is of no use to us. As long as the Romans are here, our enemies are the Romans, not the Pharisees."

I objected strongly, "But the Sanhedrin supports the Romans, derives its power from the procurator. And besides that, the Romans don't scare us. If the Rabbi gave the order to attack the Tower, the crowd would obey."

Emon, the youngest and most impetuous, decided to intervene. "So why doesn't he give the order, what's he waiting for?"

I rebutted, "And you, what are you all waiting for? Why don't you make a move? We have."

Mahat spoke again, "We want to get a clear idea of what's going on. Your Rabbi doesn't convince us."

Bitterly, I said, "The kingdom has come, and you haven't even noticed."

Ariel answered me, trying to sound friendly. "It's tough to understand what kingdom you're talking about, Judas. One minute it's here on earth, the next it's up in heaven. We have to have a sense of responsibility; a lot of men's lives depend on our command. We can't lose contact with what's real, with things as they are."

I observed, "You're reasoning like Romans, Ariel. Can't you see that?"

He replied. "Maybe. But if the Romans have managed to take over the world, it must mean that they aren't so bad at reasoning."

Mahat took the floor again, "Let's forget about these useless debates. For us the kingdom is power and now power is in the hands of the Romans. Are you willing to mount an attack on the Tower? By dawn tomorrow morning, we can mobilize four thousand zealots. If we manage to topple the Tower in four or five days, we'll have a good chance of beating the legions that will be sent here from Syria and Egypt. Tell your Rabbi to come here to make an agreement with us."

84

Mahat had said exactly what I would have said in his place, so I didn't know how to respond. I couldn't imagine the Rabbi in a meeting with them. I'd heard him talk a few times about legions of angels and devils, but never about Roman legions. The looks on the three men's faces grew more and more ironic as they waited in vain for my reply.

Just then some excited shouts and curses were heard outside the door; it was some merchants who were pushing to get in.

One of them cursed, "He's crazy, crazy! He took a whip to us! Why don't they arrest him?"

And another, "We've got to stone him. As soon as he got to the Temple, he started overturning the counters of the money changers, the stands of the merchants. I had a cage with seven doves, but he drove them away."

And yet another, "He smashed a bottle of my olive oil. Now, who's going to pay me for it?"

This was an unexpected complication, with which the three leaders seemed to be satisfied. "Sounds as though not quite all the people are following him," Emon said.

"These gentlemen are not part of the people," I shot back, irritated, and I immediately got up to go hear and see better.

One man—it wasn't certain that he was a merchant—was saying, "I don't like social disorders, people take advantage of them to steal. Jerusalem is already a den of thieves; all we need now is the Galileans."

One of the others retorted, "Listen to who's talking. You haven't done anything but steal your whole life."

Meanwhile, a group of patrons was gathering around the merchants—by now there wasn't anything interesting happening out on the street—and they were exchanging wisecracks and insults. Aser, the innkeeper, threatened, "Stay calm or I'll throw you out."

The merchant whose doves had flown away said, "This time it's not going to end here. I'm poor, don't count for much. But among the merchants there are also some who make big donations to the Temple. The priests had better know how to defend us from this crazed demoniac and his stinking followers."

A woman—women always had great sympathy for him—said in a sad voice, "What's he got to gain by taking on the powerful? He's young, he has no experience of life. He ought to know that if you go up against the powerful you lose every time."

Somebody broke in, "Who knows? Have you ever seen the people as excited as they are today? Have you ever seen them like this, ready to follow a leader? And not a Roman soldier in sight; the heroes are afraid. And what about Herod's troops? And the slaves of the Sanhedrin? They haven't made a move; they just sit there watching. I'm telling you that a man has been born of Israel."

Now everybody wanted to talk, all at once. "And if he were the Anointed? If he really were the Anointed?" "In my mind, he is." "Yes, the Anointed that wrecks my cage full of doves!" "But you, why have you made a market out of the house of the Most High?" "We pay taxes to the priests; aren't they supposed to be the priests of the Most High?" "They're thieves and servants of the Romans."

Two others came in, perhaps husband and wife. They had been onlookers, in a courtyard of the Temple, at the encounter between the Rabbi and some Greek pilgrims with whom the Rabbi had stopped to talk. The woman recounted having heard words that had made her cry. She had heard him say, "Now my spirit is uneasy. And what will I say? 'Father, free me from this hour?' But I have come for this hour."

My heart was in tumult as I listened. Maybe it was better to go to him, maybe he needed me.

But the woman's account was too fascinating. She was saying that she had heard the Rabbi say, his gaze turned to the heavens, "Father, glorify thy name." And, according to the woman, an angel had replied from the heavens, calling out loudly, "I have glorified it and I will glorify it again."

The husband did not agree. "But what angel! That was the sound of thunder!"

"As far as I'm concerned it was an angel."

"And I say it was thunder."

"You don't have faith, that's why you can't see angels. How can the Eternal help us, if we do not believe?"

The beggar who was pulling himself along on his hands said, "If I went to him and asked him: Son of David, make my legs grow, what would he do?"

A merchant answered him, "You sound like a lunatic. Do you really think that that Galilean, that raving vagabond, is capable of making legs grow?"

Somebody shouted out with animosity, "Why not? He brought Lazarus back to life when he had already started to stink!"

And the beggar, "I don't know whether to believe or not. The fact is I don't have legs. I was born without legs, do you realize that? Can I have been born with sin? My parents will have done the sinning, that they should be damned for my birth. But if it's true that this Galilean comes from God, he could give me explanations and do something for my legs."

The merchant became indignant on hearing this last speech. He pulled out a silver coin and showed it to the beggar. "It's yours, if you spit on the name of that damned Galilean."

The beggar seemed tempted, then he spit in the direction of the merchant. "There, I spit on your name, which I don't even know."

He took a couple of kicks from the infuriated merchant. But he must have been inured to getting kicked. He pulled himself up as best he could, shouting, "Barkeep! Aser! Bring me a jug of wine, a full jug! I want to get drunk for the glory of the Galilean who takes his whip to merchants!"

"Can you pay for it?" Aser asked.

The beggar rummaged through his rags and pulled out a handful of small coins, yelling, "It's Passover! A time of abundance for beggars, thieves, whores, and pimps in the city of David!"

85

Then I felt my whole body quiver; I was being pulled into action. I jumped on top of a table thrusting my fist into the air with the purse, the community purse. "Aser! Give everyone a drink! And make sure it's your best wine, for the glory of Jesus of Nazareth!"

They shouted back, "Hosanna! Hosanna! Glory on high! Glory to Jesus of Nazareth! Glory to the king of Israel!"

I felt strengthened by their fervor.

One of them said to me, "Really, will that Galilean that we saw ride by on the donkey crush the Romans, the high priests, and all their servants?"

I answered in a strong, firm voice, "The man you have seen go by on the donkey is the son of the living God. The powers of heaven and hell, angels and demons are under his command; they obey him as servants do their master. Today is a glorious day for the people of Israel. The promised kingdom has come: for all of us, sons of Abraham, there will no more misery, nor suffering. Jesus of Nazareth has said, 'those who observe my word will never see death, and those who drink the water I give them will thirst no more. . . .'"

The legless beggar, who had already had enough to drink, interrupted me, "Water, brother? Why water? Wine, to the health of the new king of the Jews!"

They applauded him and shouted hosanna to the new king of the Jews.

And I went on to talk some more, addressing myself to them, but really thinking of Mahat, Ariel, and Emon, who had not moved from their table. "You cry hosanna and hail, and that is good, as easy as it is to shout today, a day of triumph, after you have heard the rabble acclaim him, seen the walls, the streets, the very houses of Jerusalem proclaim him king and the son of David. The frightened Romans are shut inside their fortress. Pharisees, priests, and doctors of law are disoriented and divided. One day, he said unto us, 'some of those who are present here will not die until they have seen the kingdom of God arrive with all its power.' He has kept his promise: the kingdom has come; Jesus of Nazareth sits on the throne of David. There will be a reward for those who worked for his victory. Now, let's move, let's go to bring him our strength and our faith. Let us remember the words of the Book: with God we will do mighty things for he will crush our foes."

86

Amid acclamations and cheering they moved toward the door, pushing and shoving, they started making their way out. I jumped down from the table to go with them. But first I turned toward Jerusalem's best.

They were still there, sitting at their table. I said, "You, I imagine, want to see things more clearly."

"Exactly, Judas," Mahat replied. "Anyway, you know how to create enthusiasm among the people. If by chance things shouldn't end up going as you think, and you get out alive, we'll wait for you."

I was brimming with contempt. "There'll be no recompense for you in the kingdom."

"We're not looking for recompense. We'll be satisfied to see Israel free, with your Galilean on the throne. Good luck."

I started off, but before I could get to the door, I bumped into Simon who was coming toward me, breathless. "Judas, Judas, the Rabbi wants you."

I asked him out loud, so that the zealots would hear me too, "Has he already sat on the throne of the king?"

He answered, gloomily, "No. He went up to the Temple, talked with the doctors and the Pharisees, and then decided to leave for the night." Under his breath, so he wouldn't be heard by strangers, he added, "We're going to Bethany, to the house of Lazarus."

To Bethany, to the house of Lazarus? He was going to abandon Jerusalem after having it in hand? Ah, Peter, John, James! All cowards, they trembled before a servant of the Sanhedrin, and the Rabbi never strayed from them, he followed their advice, eyes closed. I shouldn't have left him alone.

I heard Emon saying in a scornful tone, "So even today, the powers that be remain the powers that be."

I turned back to them to tell them, giving it all I had to assume the serene majesty of the Rabbi, "Some of those present here will not taste death until they have seen the kingdom of God come with all its power."

I hurried to leave with Simon.

The streets of Jerusalem were already shrouded in darkness, near the doors to their houses, the daughters of Zion were lighting the brazier with which to warm themselves during the long night; the voices, the shouts, the crying of the children were the same as ever, there was the smell of food and smoke, inside the houses you could see the tenuous glimmers of light from fires or oil lamps. The city could have become a funeral pyre or a triumph, but instead it was preparing for its usual night's rest, after a day of ephemeral enthusiasm and emotion.

The procurator of Caesar and his soldiers were keeping watch over an unchanged city.

87

On the road to Bethany, a moonless night, all the experiences of the glorious day having turned into mortal dejection, I was stumbling over bushes and stones. Your words, Jesus. Your words: walk as long as you have light, until the darkness overtakes you. That is: go forward toward heaven—the kingdom whose meaning was unclear—as long as I, who am the light, am with you. As long as you have light, believe in the light and you will be sons of the light.

All fine, but I was stumbling, and thinking of Your obscure melancholy, Rabbi, from which derived my discouragement, and my weariness.

When You were sad, did you have in mind only the innocents slaughtered in Bethlehem to make Your birth memorable? Or did Your tedium of life have deeper roots, a wider meaning: a panic frustration, that encapsulated the vanity of existence? An endless void, Qohelet called it, an endless nothingness: everything is empty nothingness.

In the beginning God created heaven and earth, and that was the first deception, completed by breathing the capacity for sin and repentance into a creature formed out of dust.

Oh Rabbi Jesus, what is this bleak adventure You have dragged us into, after telling us to be happy and rejoice because great would be our recompense in the kingdom? Those who, later on, built a church on Your death, decided, after discussing it exhaustively, to put sloth among the mortal sins, the sins for which sinners lose their souls.

Well, giving in to boredom or melancholy, failing to do good while having the opportunity to do so, that is sloth. You had the kingdom in hand, and You let it go. It could also have been called betrayal. We, Your followers—they, if not me—had the right to recompense in the kingdom, just as a worker has a right to his wages. What was the sense of going up to the Temple, driving off some of the merchants, looking around, and then, the hour being late, fleeing to Bethany? Why were You afraid to stay in the city for the night? The Romans would not have come out of the tower and the Sanhedrin was more frightened than You. So, why run away?

The two main events that You had shown You were aiming at for the entire time of Your apostolate—power and death—You had discarded, for that day, and a day as favorable as that one would be very hard to come by again. Even admitting that there was danger of death—You had information that we didn't have—You, Your death, hadn't You always presented it as a means for achieving the glory that is over and above power?

You had said to us, before we set off for Jerusalem, "The son of man will soon be delivered into the hands of men." None of them meditated on the meaning of this sentence, which in any case they didn't understand. But I understood it completely. To be delivered implied that someone would have to deliver You, put You into their hands, and You were asking for complicity. It was understood that it would fall to me, and I was ready, whenever You should decide.

Right from the beginning, my devotion had been without limits. If You gave Your life for others, why should I not give my life for You, or anything else that might be asked of me?

You had claimed everything, and everything had been given You, but then, on the brink of achieving the objective, it seemed You didn't know what to do.

88

Nor had You shown that You knew what to do with the fervor of the crowd—which had even proclaimed You king and Son of God. Sure enough, the crowd, when it acclaims, acclaims first and foremost itself, so the object of its acclamations doesn't count for much, but they were acclamations that You had in many ways provoked, and perhaps even solicited and manipulated, and anyway not all the citizens of Jerusalem were sitting down to dinner under an oil lamp at this hour. Left to regret that things had gone in such an unadorned fashion there was certainly a legless drunk, and certainly some women had thought about the kingdom You had been promising as a time of personal rehabilitation, and surely a lot of children saw again in their dreams the strange figure of that king riding joylessly along on a donkey in the midst of all that glory, and without a doubt some zealots who with their men could have been ready to go into combat before dawn, were now laughing behind my back, but not without bitterness since, in any event and for everybody, an opportunity had been lost.

And now, what were we to expect now?

In Bethany they had prepared a banquet for You that resounded with echoes of the triumph of Jerusalem, as though it had been firmly established or could be easily repeated the next day. You were not in high spirits—when were You ever?—but there was good food and good wine, and You, wishing to demonstrate that becoming a follower of Yours did not necessarily mean a diet of locusts, did not disdain either the food or the wine, and there was Lazarus with his influential Judean friends whose presence was reassuring, and there was Martha, the hard-working housewife, and Mary, the adoring hostess: could this be a final goal? Who knows? Peter and John, James and Andrew, and on down the line, were not, from what could be seen, at all unsatisfied.

I didn't go in, I lay down in the portico, wrapped in my mantle, a rock for a pillow, and not even locusts for dinner. Rabbi, I didn't have any slaughtered innocents in my past; for what did I have to punish myself? Maybe for the years— by now years—spent following You, interrogating You in silence, trying to believe? You promised Yourself and others death and glory, and if it was all to end up in banquets in the house of Lazarus, nothing remained for me but pain and bewilderment.

It was a night of disquiet, with little sleep. Late, one by one, heavy of foot, others came to lie down in the portico, and they quickly fell asleep. Oh Eternal, when will it be given to me to give you back my life? Whoever speaks out against the son of man will be forgiven; I was due forgiveness. But those who will have brought offense to the holy spirit will not be forgiven. Was this my case? I could hear Your voice, Rabbi: "Do not be afraid, little flock, my father has ordained to give you the kingdom."

Why did You fall short? And how many contradictions, obscurities, uncertainties did we have before us, what was in store for us now?

89

What was in store for us were nearly senseless days.

It began with the fig tree. The next morning, intent on returning to Jerusalem, we left the house of Lazarus and, as soon as we were out of Bethany, the Rabbi was hungry. There was a fig tree in sight, and he went over to it to see if there was something to eat. The fig tree had leaves, because it was spring, but it had no figs because generally the figs come later. Having found nothing, the Rabbi was annoyed and said, "No more fruit will grow from you."

The fig tree withered completely from one moment to the next—or maybe we found it withered the next morning?—and he taught us that by praying with faith we could obtain whatever we wanted, even to move a mountain from one place to another, which is an operation almost as senseless as withering a fig tree.

Then he went up to the Temple and began teaching with precepts and parables. There were people there to hear him, not many, but enough so that the Pharisees, doctors, and priests were afraid to arrest him. But they were looking for a pretext to incriminate him and they asked him subtle questions, little traps which he was able to avoid ingeniously, responding to the questions that were supposed to embarrass him with other questions that they didn't know how to answer, or else by formulating responses that surprised them and left them unable to rebut.

They asked him: "By what authority do you teach? Does your right to teach come from God or from man?"

And the Rabbi replied, "And John, where did he get the right to baptize? From God or from man?"

In order to avoid falling into contradiction, they answered, "We don't know."

And the Rabbi, almost insolently, "Neither am I going to tell you by what right I do these things."

Then they posed him the question of a woman who had, abiding by the law, married six brothers consecutively, as each of them died. On the day of resurrection which of the six would be her husband? He was ready to ridicule them as they deserved. What was their idea of the day of resurrection? When people are resurrected on the last day, they don't take a wife or a husband, because they are like angels from heaven.

They also asked him, as a way of compromising him before the procurator, if it was licit to pay taxes to Caesar, and if they had to pay them or not. With surprising deftness, he asked for a coin and furnished a response that people all over the world would use for centuries when they needed to get out of certain tough situations.

Listening to him, even the doctors of law were forced to say, "Rabbi, you're right." And even some of the head priests believed in him, but they didn't say so publicly because of the Pharisees, who would have expelled them from the synagogue. In fact, they preferred the glory of the world to the glory of God. Did he think this was the way to take power?

Even if it had been possible, there was no continuity in his behavior.

90

There was no continuity. At times, quite unexpectedly, majesty and greatness welled up in You. You said, "Heaven and earth will pass away, but my words shall not pass away."

And again, "The son of man will come on a cloud, with great splendor and power."

In Your words, time was all mixed together, past and future blended with the present; You spoke of certain things, and it wasn't clear if You were thinking of them as already having happened in the Book, or about to happen, or destined to happen at the end of time. "The Eternal is not a God of the dead, but of the living," You said, and among the living You listed Abraham, Isaac, and Jacob, all dead for centuries.

At times Your voice returned to sounding like an impetuous wind: woe to you, doctors and hypocritical Pharisees, who include in the offering to the Lord all the way down to the last hundredth of a cent while you neglect to include law, mercy, and fidelity. "Woe to you, blind guides, who say: if one swears by the Temple, it means nothing but if one swears by the gold of the temple, then it counts. Woe to you, who shut the gates of the kingdom of heaven in people's faces, who journey by land and by sea to make one proselyte, and then make him twice as worthy of the inferno as yourselves. Whited sepulchers, woe to you! You raise funeral monuments to the prophets that your ancestors killed, and so you acknowledge that you are the descendants of murderers and prophets. Throw yourselves down, serpents, poisonous reptiles. Now it is your turn. Come, complete in me the work of your ancestors! Then Your mind returned to the fate of Jerusalem, as it often did in those days. There shall not be left here one stone upon another, You said, and it wasn't clear which was greater, the sadness or the satisfaction for the terrible misfortunes that would befall the children of those who afflicted You with pain and persecution. The city that killed prophets and persecuted the envoys of God would pay for its faults with tremendous destruction: not one stone upon another, everything demolished.

When would it happen? When you see Jerusalem surrounded by armies, then you will know that its destruction is near. Those will be the days of the vendetta in which all of the prophecies will be fulfilled.

91

Sometimes, Your discourse addressed a more distant time, the final events: nation shall rise up against nation and kingdom against kingdom. A brother will consign his brother to death, a father will consign his son, children will revolt against their parents to have them put to death. There will be earthquakes in various diverse localities and there will be death from starvation. Then let them who are in Judea flee to the mountains and let them who are on the terrace not come down and enter the house to get something, and let them who are in the fields not turn back to get their mantles. Woe to women with child, in those days, and to mothers suckling their children. After these tribulations, the heavens will grow dark and the moon will cease to shine, and the stars will start falling from the sky, and the powers of the heavens shall be shaken.

Was all this fantasizing about distant terrors not an expedient for taking Your mind off more imminent terrors, a way of delaying a little more the hour for which You had come?

In effect, it was a way to buy time, a fence straddling that Luke synthesized in the phrase: and during the day he was teaching in the Temple, but at night he went out and spent the night on the mount known as the Mount of Olives.

What were You missing? What incitement or help? Surely, You had no use for the crowd that, after acclaiming You the king awaited for centuries, went home to sit down at table, nor did You need Peter with his ridiculous sword and his spirit inclined to deny You at the slightest adversity, and not even John and Mary of Bethany, who would have given their lives for You with ardor, but uselessly, as the zealots observed.

What then, could have been useful to You? Not sacrifices, but mercy, You had said one day, and never was it sufficiently clear what was to be understood by mercy. Perhaps a more conscious and constructive participation in what we could give You; a communion, I sometimes hoped. Did You also want acceptance of the resurrection, of Lazarus and Your own?

I was anxious to do Your will, but You never looked at me in those days. Were You afraid that You would see in my eyes a reminder of Your promises and duties?

Yes, there was disappointment and reproof in me, but there was also desire for comfort—for faith, finally—and instead You left me to torment myself in search of a meaning for the word mercy, for a reason to Your verb: "I am." Perhaps it wasn't a present but a becoming, and not only Yours, but necessarily of many, if not everyone, all of humanity. You had gone way beyond the prophets of the Book, but this was yet to be fulfilled, nor could I manage to imagine how it could be done. I understood only that You were searching on earth for another kind of involvement, some support that was still missing. But what, what? Can I? Me?

There is no call for my impatience.

I implore You; hurry up and answer me, O Eternal One of my pain.

92

Then, everything was set in motion with smooth simplicity when, on the first day of the unleavened bread, on the occasion of the paschal sacrifice, we asked him, "Rabbi, where do you want us to go to prepare dinner so that you can eat the paschal supper?"

You said to prepare in the city.

So we were to remain in town that night, and I felt that finally my hour too had come. I had a presentiment; some things had already happened that predisposed me to the complicity that he would ask of me.

One day, on which my disappointment at the Rabbi's indecision was rather evident—we were in the first courtyard of the Temple—I was approached by a man who was poorly dressed, almost as a beggar. I had already seen him among the patrons in Aser's tavern on the day of our entrance into Jerusalem. He too was shouting hosanna but not with the same passion as the others. There was something equivocal about him, one might have thought he was one of the Sanhedrin's many spies.

In fact, he was. He had said to me, "My name is Asaf. In case you feel the need to talk with someone from the Sanhedrin, even with the high priest himself, I can help you. I live right in front of Aser's tavern."

I hadn't given him an answer, nor had I looked at him; he should have understood that I didn't want to be importuned.

Instead, he insisted, "I have approached you because you are a Judean from Jerusalem, you know the scriptures, you were with the zealots when you were younger. The others don't understand a thing. The leaders don't want to kill your prophet, nor hurt him. They just want him to go away and never come back again. Try to get him to understand that before the Sanhedrin lose their patience."

He wasn't a servant, maybe he was a leader, a doctor demoted to a spy. I replied, "The Rabbi knows what he wants to do, and anyway none of us is capable of giving him advice. But don't count on his going back to Galilee. He has come for this hour, whatever might be its value."

This had happened in the first courtyard of the Temple— the Rabbi was debating with the doctors of law as to whether the Anointed was to be considered a son of David or not—and more than a few of his disciples had had the chance to see me as I was speaking with a Judean who could easily have been taken for a spy. It might even have been the case that Asaf, before he approached me, had approached one of them.

This may have been what gave rise to the rumors which, passing from mouth to mouth, were later written down as history.

93

Here, for example, is how Luke tells it.

"The high priests and the doctors of law were still looking for a way to eliminate him, because they were afraid of the people. So, Satan entered into the heart of Judas known as Iscariot, one of the group of twelve. He went off by himself to come to terms with the head priests and the command of the guard as to the way he could deliver him up to them. They were very satisfied and promised to repay him in money. Judas accepted and began looking for the right opportunity to deliver him to them without the people noticing."

It is a bare-bones, precise account, which, however, does not recount the truth—the truth in which there is the weight of human feelings is never so compact or simple—instead it bears witness to the rumors, by then crystalized by the years, around a betrayal.

Equally conventional are the accounts of Mark and Matthew: their Judas does not have the complexity of a man, but the abstractness of a symbol; namely, the symbol of evil.

Here's Mark: "Judas Iscariot, one of the twelve, went to the high priests to deliver up Jesus. They were delighted by the news and promised to give him money. As for Judas, he looked for the opportunity to betray him."

Matthew's narrative is nearly as brief, but it specifies that I supposedly asked the high priests, "How much are you willing pay me if I deliver him to you?" And they, referring to a passage from Ezekiel which had nothing to do with the negotiation in progress, fixed the sum at thirty coins of silver, and these thirty dinars have entered into the language of almost all the nations of the earth to signify infamy.

So. It is recounted by Matthew, Mark, and Luke, with the same haste, almost with the same exact words, placing the negotiation for the betrayal in the days in which the Rabbi was waggling with the doctors and the Pharisees in the courtyards of the Temple. But neither Matthew nor Mark nor Luke were there in those days, none of them had seen Jesus personally, all they could do was collect rumors.

John, however, was there, and with the anguished separation drawing near, he was the closest to the Rabbi, to him it was permitted. So John knew things that others did not know, even the perturbation of Jesus for the role he had designated for me, and reporting his last words—when it was already clear to him that glory was death, and his death the inevitable heart of the things created and of the creator himself—testified that he had said to the father, "As long as I was with them I maintained them in your name that you gave to me, and I protected them and none of them was lost, except the son of perdition, so that he could fulfill the scripture."

94

Perhaps, Rabbi, if Your glory had been achieved, You would have redeemed me from the sin of a betrayal which derived— it can be understood—from origin and scripture. But things went differently, and the role of the traitor without redemption was left to me, but no one considers the way in which I came to betray You, because John, who knew everything because he never left Your side in those last days, recounted the facts, but not all of them honestly.

Indeed, this is the way his account of the Last Supper begins:

"Before the feast of Passover, knowing that the time had come for him to pass from this world to the father, Jesus, who had loved his followers who were in the world, loved them until the very end." I was one of Yours, and I know that in a certain way I too was loved, and perhaps even more, until the very end, but John, who hated me, hastened, in his account, to exclude me from Your love, "During the meal, when Satan had already entered the heart of Judas Iscariot, son of Simon, to betray him. . . ."

That's not true. Up to a certain point of the supper, there was no betrayal in my soul, but only the desperate resignation to do whatever You should command me to do. John knew this well, and he knew when, how and why Satan—the idea of the betrayal, the duty to carry it out—entered my heart. He recounted it; he had to. But he did it with such confusion that everyone continued to believe that Judas, infamy of the human race, had voluntarily betrayed his Rabbi, son of God, God.

I am the darkness, Jesus. But of You, who are the light, I continue to ask, from the depths of my darkness: in the story of Your death which was supposed to be glory and victory over death, was I, Judas, marked by You as the son of perdition, simply an instrument so that the scripture should be fulfilled, that is, that the mysterious will of the Eternal should be done? Or rather, was there something that we had in common, something that, seeing how things went, was not fulfilled, if not in the lesser conclusion that the both of us died almost together?

Perhaps, Rabbi, our greatness was destined for more modest ends. But once it was decided that the final objective was to be glory, it was not I who fell short.

95

The instructions for preparing the supper were, as often happened with us even for the most ordinary things, unthinkably minute and abstruse; was there really so much danger that we had to be cautious as snakes? The disciples didn't seem to have dramatic presentiments, nor did they appear to be preoccupied any more than is to be expected for a normal paschal supper. But the Rabbi had to follow ways that sometimes had to do with the scriptures, and other times satisfied a need for mystery, or ritual, something more than mere prudence.

Anyway, he called the two disciples whom he trusted the most for everyday things—Peter and John, of course—and gave the orders: "As soon as you enter the city, you will be met by a person carrying a pitcher of water. Follow her, and to the owner of the house where she enters, you shall say, 'The Rabbi asks you, "where is the room where he can eat the paschal supper with his disciples?" He will show you a large upstairs room, furnished with rugs and cushions. Prepare there.'"

Had everything already been arranged earlier—more or less as the resurrection of Lazarus—or was this some arcane clairvoyance that reached down to even the meanest details? Or was it the father who took care of such trifling matters, leaving no margin for surprises or mishaps, nor, in the end, any freedom for merit or fault. Did a betrayal, in such a context, have other obligations apart from those that may have been pre-established by scripture? Was there, in the soul of the Rabbi, any real possibility of not going through with it, or even to go ahead in a somewhat different way than that which seemed to have been so meticulously predisposed?

The bad habit of asking questions can get worse when you're referred to as the son of perdition.

96

In any event, on entering the city, Peter and John found everything just as the Rabbi had said, and they prepared the supper. Then they came back to let us know that everything had gone for the best and so, when evening fell, we set off for the designated house. We stretched out on the cushions haphazardly, each of us contesting the other for the most favorable place, but in the end respecting a hierarchy that had been established over time. To the right of the Rabbi sat James, then Andrew, Bartholomew, and Thomas. On his left, protected by benevolence, the young lad John. Peter sat opposite him—the plates with the food were set out in the middle—and I was next to Peter, and the Rabbi's gaze, that night, sometimes met mine, with no preoccupation of finding reproof or solicitation. Both of us knew that the time had come for him to pass from this world to the father, and the awareness of this gave a sweet spirituality to his melancholy. He loved us. He had loved us until then and he loved us to the end, and—that night—he loved one more than the others, and, despite all of his holding his head against his heart, it was not John. At last, our hour had come.

He said, "I ardently desired to share this paschal supper with you before suffering, because, believe me, I will not eat it again until it is fully realized in the kingdom of heaven."

They showed no understanding. It had always happened that they understood very little, and the fact that they now understood nothing was of no importance; at present they were not necessary to him. He had come from God and to God he was to return, and if there were scriptures to be observed for the suffering of that passage, there was one who had made the commitment to lend himself; he could not be doubted.

Nevertheless, although, as far as it appeared, the event was to come about within the confines of that night, at the moment, there was no urgency; things had to unfold with ritual heartrending torment. So, before touching food, he got up, laid aside his mantle, took a cloth and tied it around his waist, poured some water in a basin, and began washing the feet of his disciples, starting with James who was on his right, and then one by one the others, who, though aghast, let him proceed.

But when it was his turn, Peter could not refrain from exhibiting himself in one of his scenes, "You, lord, washing my feet?"

The Rabbi replied patiently, "Now you do not know what I am doing, but later you will understand."

Peter insisted, proclaiming that he would never permit his lord to wash his feet, and so the Rabbi cut him short, "If I do not wash your feet, you will have no part with me."

He surrendered with ridiculous frenzy, "If that's the way it is, Lord, not only my feet, but also my hands and my head."

That would have been overdoing it, and in fact the Rabbi objected that if one has already had a bath, he has no need to wash again, since, apart from his feet, the rest is already pure.

Even admitting that this talk had some esoteric meaning, it was getting long and drawn out, and it was by no means clear how something could come of it that had anything to do with the imminent hour. But then the Rabbi, looking at us one by one—already washed—said, "And you are all pure." He said it just like that, but immediately he seemed to have second thoughts, lowered his eyes and keeping them low, that is, without looking at anyone in particular, he added in a whisper, "But not all of you."

Many of the Rabbi's words fell into the void because they weren't understood or weren't heard. But John, so close to his lips—in the meantime the Rabbi had returned to his place—clearly understood the words he had said—"But not all of you"—and then he wrote that he had said them thinking of me who was about to betray him. But nothing proves that he was actually thinking of me. There were others, John included, who, a little later on, when asked to pray and keep vigil over a deathly sadness, would repeatedly fall asleep. Not to mention one who during that night—a night of anguish in which Satan had asked to have us at his disposal to sift us as one does with grain—would deny him three times.

97

Rabbi, in that little flock that was about to be dispersed, there were several of us with scabs of impurity. Anyway, whether pure or impure, You washed all of our feet and You explained, "Have you understood what I have done? You call me Rabbi and Lord, and that is well, because I am. If then I, who am Lord and Rabbi, have washed your feet, you must also wash each other's feet. I have given you an example."

Then, with a majesty never before seen on Your face, You took a piece of bread, broke it and, after giving thanks, gave each of us a piece of it, saying, "Take this and eat it for this is my body."

We ate the bread.

Then You raised a chalice of wine, gave thanks to the Eternal, and gave it to us to drink from it. And we passed it from one to another, each drinking a sip, as You said, "What you are drinking is my blood, the blood of the covenant, which is shed for you and for the multitude. I shall drink no more the fruit of the vine until the day I shall drink it again in the kingdom of God."

You thus made, if only symbolically, a gift of Yourself, body and blood, but no one made much of it, nor asked for explanations. They didn't even notice that by this time Your talk of death was referred to an event that was very close, it may have already been past the hour. The son of man was going away, as it was written of him, but it might be that small delays were still permitted; there were formalities to observe, moments to be taken advantage of, choices to be confirmed.

Again, You turned to us, repeating to each and everyone Your love and, with all of the uncertainty and obtuseness that might still be in our souls, trust. Indeed, You said, "I know whom I have chosen."

But immediately afterwards You added, "Nevertheless, the word of the scripture must be carried out. One who eats the bread with me has raised his heel against me."

Words of a great king from our history. He had pronounced them when he was already in decline, overcome with fear, torn by thoughts of persecution, sick with remorse for his sins. Why did You choose to say those words? Was there no other way to illustrate the necessity for a betrayal? Or did You want to emphasize that he who had been commanded to turn his back on You was one with whom You had lived in peace, in whom You had confided? Surely, if it was me You spoke of, You could be trusting; I would not fail You.

You were so sure of it, You said, "I tell you now before it happens, so that when it happens you will know that I am."

This could have been a key to understanding for the future, the ignominy of a betrayal for the benefit of Your becoming.

And then You added a sentence—everything was tremendously important on that occasion—a sentence that appeared to have nothing to do with what had been said up to then, but that perhaps had secret pertinence in relation to one who would soon be going to Caiaphas to take payment of the small price of a great betrayal, and even with respect to Caiaphas himself, who by paying thirty dinars would take part in a necessary and universal event.

You said, "He who welcomes him whom I have sent welcomes me and he who welcomes me welcomes him who sent me."

98

Now, Jesus, there was no more time to be wasted. Having established the sacredness of the betrayal, with no further delays or hesitations You had to send someone, designate the accomplice. This hour could not be allowed to pass, nor the verb "I am" wait for fulfillment. You were overcome with intense emotion and in the end, You said, "Verily I say to you, one of you shall betray me."

The announcement surprised them. You had pre-announced the betrayal more than once: You had even referred to it moments before with words of David—the words of David would soon come back in You again to denounce another and definitive abandonment—yet they were dumbfounded as though it were something new, and then they began to look at one another, not knowing of whom You had spoken. One of you, You had said, and in their view it could have been any one of us, they had no idea what a terrible greatness was to befall him who had been designated to pay a price much harsher than death. They kept on asking themselves who among them was about to do such a thing.

You were absorbed in deep sadness, and You held close to You him whom You had allowed to share even Your sadness. John, in fact, leaned his head against Your breast.

And Peter, who was more than anyone else—perhaps not without reason and fear—anxious to know, signaled to John to ask You whom You were referring to.

And John, pressing in even closer to You, asked, "Lord, who is it?"

I heard his question, and also Your answer.

You responded, "It is he to whom I shall offer the morsel I am about to dip."

The plates where everyone dipped their bread were in the middle of the table, according to our custom, and now You had to make the elementary and final gesture of taking a piece of bread, dipping it, and then offering it to one of us, the designated one. Afterwards, there would be no turning back, even for You.

99

You then took a morsel of bread—very slowly—You dipped it in a plate—even more slowly—and I knew it was for me—it was not everyone who could do what would be asked of me to do, and I too had an hour for which I had come—and yet I continued to pray that—if possible—the chalice would be taken from me. The morsel had now been dipped. You could have offered it to Peter, or to John, or to any other of the twelve; everything, in a certain sense, was still to be decided.

Leaning forward, avoiding my eyes, You offered it to me, Judas of Simon Iscariot, son of perdition.

The others, distant or distracted, didn't notice a thing. But John was right there, leaning on Your breast, hearing Your every word and breath, observing every expression and gesture, even the smallest. And, many years later, John wrote, "In that moment, after the morsel, Satan entered his heart."

They are words of the Holy Spirit: in that moment, after the morsel that You had given me as a commandment.

Still, overwhelmed, I hesitated, I needed confirmation and exhortation. So You said to me, "What you are about to do, do quickly."

None of the others, aside from John, understood the significance of what You said. They thought that, since I kept the purse, You had ordered me to go buy something, or to give something to the poor. We were alone in our mission, and You urged me to act quickly because, by now, the less time was wasted the better, for both of us.

John wrote, "Judas, then, after having taken the morsel, left. And it was night."

It was, indeed, a pitch-black night; the Eternal had hidden the face of the new moon behind a veil of clouds.

100

The rest of it, if we're talking about acts to be done, actions to be carried out, was not hard.

I went to Asaf, who took me to Caiaphas, who presented me to the council, which was meeting in permanent session to come up with a way to resolve, without resentment among the people, the issue of that Galilean come to disturb the public order, and perhaps even a conscience or two.

It was written that someone would deliver him, and I pronounced myself willing to deliver my Rabbi, Jesus of Nazareth. I would deliver him that same night, if they so pleased; as for me, the sooner the better. They believed me, they paid me right away with a sum that, for some ancient and incomprehensible reason, was thirty dinars. They told me to go and wait under the portico in the first courtyard of the Temple.

There were lighted torches in the first courtyard, with large shadowy areas between one torch and another. I chose the darkest corner. Afterwards, guards started coming in, and Judeans armed with swords, lances, clubs. I was thinking that every human being—or only some—has their verb— I am—to fulfill, great or miserable as it may be, divine or demoniac. I was just about to fulfill mine—demoniac: all that was left for me to do was to lead to the agreed-upon place a crowd of armed Judeans who, on their own, wouldn't have had the courage to put their hands on a harmless Galilean.

Then it would be up to You, Rabbi, to bring to fruition Your divine verb; to be the Anointed, the Messiah of the Messiahs, the Redeemer of the human race.

I, at last, believed.

101

Words of Qoheleth: but there is no man on earth capable of doing good without doing evil. Perhaps the Eternal had also ordained the contrary, that there was no capacity to do evil without doing good. I was—I would be eternally—the loneliest man in all of humanity, the son of perdition. In a pitch-black courtyard, by now with few questions left in my soul, I was waiting to carry out my ignominious duty.

Nevertheless, despite the great malaise that weighed upon me, I felt that he, the betrayed Rabbi, was the Anointed, promised and come, final terminus of our sacred history, which began from God. Through him, the day in which the Eternal had created the earth and the heavens would re-emerge from the impenetrable depths of mystery. Through him, meaning would be given to the act of breathing a living soul into a handful of dust. The motivation and the end of all this would be manifested—or forever annulled—in his imminent glory, which could also mark the end of time, or the beginning of time finally purified of sin and fear. Earth incinerated or return to the Garden of Eden; anyway, no more inanity and pain of living, no more anguish of death, no more unlimited quantity of miseries looming over human existence. All resolved, for everyone, and forever. I alone condemned and damned for this, so this would come about.

He knew that his glory would also be owed to what I paid in ignominy and eternal damnation.

The first words he said, after I left the room in obedience to his command to act quickly, were, "Now the son of God has been glorified and God has been glorified in him. If God has been glorified in him, God in turn will glorify him in himself and he shall glorify him at once."

Obscure words, but tied to my betrayal if only by his need for me, of the one who came last, who had always been kept apart, who would not participate in all that glorification. But, as far as I was concerned, it was also possible that I should desire to find in his glorification, and not in thirty mysterious dinars, the recompense for my betrayal.

My enchantment was becoming faith; even to me they were starting to give.

102

But we are spared no maleficence, and we had a tough God, who imposed harsh conditions.

Your solitude, there in the room where You remained with the eleven, was no less miserable than mine, as I stood in a dark corner of the first court, waiting until there gathered enough armed men for an enterprise which required no arms.

John has reported the words You said that night after I had left, and they were the most high-sounding, tender, and emotional words said by You in the years of Your mission.

Your words had small-minded listeners. You gave Your heart, no one seemed worthy of receiving it, and perhaps You missed me, nor could the thought have abandoned You that I was then committing the ignominy that You had required of me. Having removed the fear of the solicitation and reproof that could be seen in my gaze, my betrayal being a condition of Your accomplishment, the hour could not be postponed, but all this did not happen without anguish.

You said, "My children, yet a little while I shall remain with you, and where I am going You cannot come."

Solitude worse than mine. Events beyond measure were happening before the eyes of the remaining eleven, and they could not see them. Luke recounts that that evening, after

You declared that someone would betray You, a dispute broke out among them about who should be considered the leader. It had to be Peter, naturally. He understood less than any of them, and his spirit, so steadfast when it came to words, was closing in on a useless betrayal.

So they were, just as You had chosen them. In no way would they participate in Your passion.

"Where I am going, you cannot come," You said, speaking of death and glory.

And Peter, "Lord, where are you going?"

"Where I am going now, you cannot follow me."

He was increasingly confused. "Lord, why cannot I follow you now? With you I am ready to confront even prison and death."

He was ready to lie. That same night, confronted by some servants, three times he would deny knowing You.

You called them Your children. Wasted love can be more heartrending than a prescribed betrayal. In Your mind, I was always the first.

Thomas, perhaps the most ingenuous, said, "Lord, we don't know where you are going, how can we find the way?"

You responded with wasted words, "I am the way, the truth, and the life, no one comes unto the father except through me. If you have known me, you shall also know my father. And from now on you know him, and you have seen him."

I had already taken—by that hour—my thirty dinars, but You were still searching among the most faithful for the proceeds of the already begun sacrifice.

Philip asked You, "Lord, show us your father and that will suffice."

This sounded very much like the way the philistines of the Temple spoke. You had been with them such a long time and they had not gotten to know You; all those professions of faith, empty words.

"Believe me, I am in the father and the father is in me."

If for nothing else, for Your works—the innumerable prodigies performed right before their eyes—they should have believed. Instead, they had no idea of what believing means; now that the hour had come.

They wanted to see with the eyes of the flesh; where was the father, that they might touch him?

103

You could already see, Rabbi, in what anguished isolation You would suffer Your passion. Where was the involvement, everyone's active participation, the common becoming? You were alone and in that fearful night, time could not be stopped; Satan had his dark rights.

You said, "I will not talk very much with you, because the prince of this world is about to come. Against me, he can do nothing, but the world must know that I love my father, and I do what my father has bid me to do."

You were already searching for comfort in Your solitude.

One day You had said that the father never abandoned You because You always did the things that pleased him. Now and forever, You obeyed Your father; therefore, he did not forsake You. How could he forsake You if the two of you were one thing? Their foolishness—prelude to defection— could grieve You, not worry You. They did not seem guilty to You, anyway they were superfluous. You had compassion for them; they should not be anxious, nor sad. It was for their good that You should go to Your father, because if You did not go first to Your father, the consoler would not descend upon them, the holy spirit of truth and understanding, of which they were in need.

"I still have many things to tell you, but now you cannot understand."

They would understand afterwards, when the spirit descended. For the moment, talking to them was wasted breath, better to get it over with, as You had also urged me to do.

"Yet a little while, and you will no longer have me with you."

You urged them to at least love one another because there were dark times ahead, for which they did not seem to be well prepared.

"Behold, the hour is coming, has already come, that you shall be dispersed in all directions, and you shall leave me alone. But I am not alone; my father is with me. I tell you this to give you peace. You must suffer in the world, but take courage, I have vanquished the world."

From what dismay did the obstinate affirmation arise in You: my father is with me; my father will not forsake me? From what tremendous uncertainty the stalwart declaration: I have vanquished the world?

104

Then, lifting Your eyes to heaven, You said in prayer, "Father, glorify Your son, so that he will glorify You. Eternal life consists in this: that they should know you, the one true God, and Your envoy, Jesus the Anointed. I have glorified You in the world, having completed the work that You had entrusted to me. And now, father, glorify me in Yourself with the glory that I had in You even before the world came to be. I have manifested Your name to those you have given me from the world; they were Yours, You gave them to me, and they have obeyed your word. I pray for those who believe. I do not pray for the world, but I pray for those that You gave me. Holy father. I am no longer in the world, but they remain in the world while I come to You. Holy father, conserve them in Your name, so they shall be one, like us. I have given them Your word, and the world has hated them because they are not of the world, as I am not of the world. I do not pray that You should take them from the world, but that You should preserve them from the spirit of evil. And I do not pray to You only for them, but also for all of those who believe in me by means of their word; that all should be one, like You, father, are in me and I in You, that they too should be one in us."

Rabbi, Jesus, I was not in Your prayer, I had had a different life experience, so that the scripture would be fulfilled. My becoming was to be the son of perdition.

By now, there had gathered around the son of perdition a sufficient number of armed men. The new moon having set, the night dark, it was time to go. Of the things prescribed, there was still one left for me to carry out: to deliver You.

Then I would await, with my death, Your glory, and I didn't know what it was nor in what it might consist. But You were, and You would make it manifest.

105

The supper over, they sang, as is the custom for the paschal celebration, hymns of thanksgiving.

Not to us, Eternal, not to us but to your name give glory. I love the Eternal because he heard my voice and my supplications. The Eternal is merciful and just.

Other words as well, a bit removed from the tradition, but certainly pertinent: I shall drink the chalice of salvation and I shall invoke the name of the Eternal. I shall honor my vows to the Eternal, and I shall do it in the presence of his people, in the courtyards of the house of the Eternal; in the midst of you, O Jerusalem.

Alleluia.

He left the house of the supper and went with his disciples across the river Kidron, toward a garden called Gethsemane, which they knew well.

Alleluia.

Soon thereafter, from the courtyards of the house of the Eternal, I set off for the same place, leading a swarm of armed men, who had been joined at the last minute by high priests, commandants of the guard, and elders. After all, the man to be arrested was not just anybody; he claimed to be sent by God, and for some days now he had been causing the Sanhedrin more than a few quandaries. We proceeded without order, with torches and lanterns, shouts and calls, the winter stars moving downward in the dark sky.

Meanwhile, the Rabbi had come to the garden. He said to his disciples, "Sit here while I go over there to pray."

But his solitude must have felt overwhelming, so he changed his mind and took with him his dearest: John, of course, and Peter and James. They were supposed to be worthy of the succor that was being asked of them. To them, transforming himself before them on the hilltop, he had shown a flash of his glory, they had been witness to his connection to the father and the great prophets.

He needed them because his anguish had become oppressive. He told them so, with humility, "My spirit is deathly sad, stay here and keep vigil with me."

He took just a few steps away from them, knelt with his face to the ground, full of questions in the face of his reality test. Probably he too had to come to terms with what was written and prescribed. He told himself, the prince of the world has no power over me. He told himself, I have vanquished the world. He told himself, I shall drink the chalice of salvation.

And his spirit remained deathly sad.

He prayed, "Father, if it is possible take this chalice away from me."

But was this not the hour for which he had come?

He hurried to add, "Father, yet not my will but yours be done."

They were one, how come the disagreement? How did he want it to happen? In a different way, or not at all? The anguish was unbearable, the solitude overwhelming.

He got up to seek comfort from the three most beloved, there just a few steps away. He found them sleeping. He didn't have the heart to reprimand John, so young, but to

Peter he said with intense bitterness, "Why? Are you unable to watch with me even for an hour? Watch and pray, to avoid falling into the temptation of sleep. I know that your spirit is willing, but the flesh is weak."

Their spirit was weak too: they fell back asleep immediately.

And the Rabbi, in desolate solitude, went back to prostrate himself with his face to the ground, tormenting himself in the struggle for acceptance of a sacrifice that he had sought so steadfastly, even sacrificing others. He prayed, with almost the same words as before, "Father, if it is not possible that this chalice be taken from me without my drinking from it, let thy will be done."

It was resignation; he would do what his father wanted, but how painful glory must have seemed to him in that moment.

I, in that moment, had already left Jerusalem with his enemies, to whom I would deliver him as established, but I too was not without anguish, and I too was doing the will of others.

His chalice, he convinced himself, he would have to drink, and again he got up to seek consolation from his three favorites, and again he found them sleeping.

Let them sleep, they were useless anyway, and it was necessary that he learn that his last endeavor, chosen or imposed, would be harder than what he had hoped or foreseen.

But his vows to the Eternal—even if the Eternal did not seem to be giving a merciful response to his prayers—he would nonetheless carry out, in the presence of all the people, in the middle of Jerusalem.

Voices could already be heard, and torches and lanterns could be seen among the trunks and branches of the olive trees. Then—perhaps he didn't want me to see how his most loved had abandoned him—he woke the sleepers, "Get up, hurry, he who betrays me is near."

106

I was in fact nearby, I even heard his voice, bitter and brusque. The disciples who were farther away also came to him. He had them all around him, uncertain and lost, some so afraid they appeared resolved to do something extreme.

But we two knew there was no possibility of conflict, nor of variations. We had to enact an event that was already written, both of us being in need of a monstrous innocence, or of an even more monstrous unconsciousness.

I glimpsed him in the smoky light of the torches. He was beautiful, he the most beautiful of men. It was known that I would have him be recognized by an embrace. "Rabbi," I said to him, and I embraced him.

It was my final duty of love, and what was to happen afterwards would give it explanation and justification, would make it enter into glory as a necessity and little did it matter that I was destined to pay for it with damnation.

He started to say, "My friend, for what you have come to do. . . ."

He couldn't complete the sentence—would he have said, for what you have come to do, I thank you? Or I bless you? Or I condemn you?—because they put their hands on him. One of the disciples—Peter? Who else?—with a move as sudden as it was ridiculous, struck one of the servants with the flat part of his sword, nearly detaching his ear.

The Rabbi—what was happening was humiliating—reprimanded him, "Do you think I couldn't ask for help from my father, who would instantly send me twelve legions of angels?"

Perhaps, in that moment, no one still had enough faith to believe in the legions of angels, but even so neither was a rusty old sword, clumsily wielded, worthy of reliance.

Anyway, there were the scriptures, and the Rabbi recalled them, explaining that with violence—celestial or terrestrial—observance would not be given to the prophecies, according to which things had to happen just as they were happening.

But they were bitter occurrences, even a bit grotesque, to be more fully tragic.

Turning to the leaders of those who had arrested him, the Rabbi said, "You have come armed with swords and clubs as though you were hunting an outlaw. Yet every day I was with you in the Temple and you didn't dare touch me. But all of this has come about in fulfillment of what was written by the prophets."

Twice, almost consecutively, in that desperate passage that concluded his difficult struggle for acceptance, he had spoken of the inevitability that it should happen according to what had been established by the father in the infinity of time. He always did what pleased his father; he would not be abandoned.

Then he concluded, saying, "But this is your hour under the dominion of the powers of darkness."

Was he trying, with these words addressed also to me, to cast my betrayal back into the sphere of responsible and therefore punishable acts? Was this his concise dismissal, after I had maintained my commitments, and had now to take myself out of history?

He let himself be bound and taken away without another word.

His disciples had already fled into the darkness a while ago, leaving him alone.

107

The death by crucifixion of a restive and enigmatic Galilean—
Your death, Rabbi—having come to pass in the times of the
Roman emperor Tiberius Claudius Nero, under the jurisdiction of the procurator for Judea Pontius Pilate—concrete
and banal references in such a fanciful episode—became,
without the presentiment of anyone involved—if not You,
if not I?—the most important episode of the entire history
of humanity, and not only for the innumerable other deaths
that followed from it, but also because the religions that
were born afterwards, perhaps in opposition to Yours, always
had in them a particle—a mustard seed that sometimes
failed to sprout—of Yours.

Your doctrine, confused and contradictory, always in
uneasy balance between heaven and earth, freedom and
destiny, expressed better than any other an unfulfilled aspiration of the human species: to carry on with the pain of living, searching for something to mitigate it, and even better
to make it cease: love, justice, equality, but above all glory,
the end of time, universal death.

You had prayed: that all should be one, like You, father,
You are in me and I in You, that even they should be one
in us. Every faith, even the most materialistic, is nour-
ished by the hope of living, or of dying, in others; cosmic

sublimation. You gave to this hope its highest, but also its most vain and difficult, expression. The uncertain results charged the meaning of Your end with excessive mystery, and it is not clear whether there prevailed in You the impulses of death, or those of love, which is life.

Was it, Your death, sacrifice or murder? Strangely, the religion that was born from You and which is named for You, and which still continues on earth its grandiose and troubled existence, insists on teaching that it was both things together, without taking into much account that in one interpretation there is more love, and in the other more hate. By the same token, it must be conceded that the disciples—those who came afterward—molded the words and facts of Your life according to convenience and not according to truth, or even rationality, and anyway it's not always easy to find rationality in mysteries.

Nevertheless, some have tried.

Friedrich Engels, one of the prophets of a new religion that—with the help of more than a few of Your disciples— is supplanting Yours, wrote, "Christianity, like all other revolutionary movements, was shaped by the masses. It was born in Palestine, in a manner completely unknown to us, at a time in which new sects, new religions, and new prophets were cropping up by the hundreds. Indeed, it is a sort of 'median' that arose spontaneously from the mutual friction of the most progressive of those sects, and was subsequently constituted in doctrine with the addition of the theories of the Alexandrine Jew Philo and, later, of strong Stoic influences."

He was not very sensitive to the proposition "I am," Friedrich Engels, not even as a hypothesis of becoming, yet, faced with the issues posed by Your way of dying—he calls it sacrifice—he says that it is like something that derives from

Your intimate essence, and this, Marxistically speaking, doesn't mean anything, because intimate essence either comes from God—and in that case we're completely off the track—or it comes from environmental and psychological influences, which, with respect to such an important question, it would be well to illustrate.

At the same time, no religion has ever been able to disentangle itself from the confusion between human and divine motivation: human motivations are all debatable while divine motivations just are, but by mystical power, and so they could just as well not be.

Another prophet, of a religion which, however, has not quite achieved the success of others—his name is Wilhelm Reich—spoke of Your death, defining it in no uncertain terms as murder, but adding to murder the germ of an enigma, and that is, an almost irrational will to kill that a society affected by emotional plague—doctors of law, Pharisees, priests and sexophobes, reactionaries and capitalists—has with respect to those who personify the life force. You, according to Reich, were—notwithstanding that Your sexual position is even more obscure than all the rest—a life force, and so the emotional plague eliminated You, by way of murder.

No one has any foundation for either completely accepting or rejecting the ideas of Doctor Reich—who by the way was also murdered by the emotional plague—but Your case, Jesus, is much more complicated.

Indeed, it happens that the life force which You personify is, in the final analysis, a death force; the only life is eternal life.

108

The mysteries that had accompanied You from birth up to Your triumphant entrance into Jerusalem, multiply and thicken step by step as the end draws near. Everything is known, everything is recounted with sufficient detail and agreement by at least four biographers, yet the conclusions they draw remain confused, almost contaminated by a lack of charity, by which good and evil, light and darkness, God and Satan, heaven and hell—You Jesus and me Judas—remain oppositional and separate, conceived in a way that is not the way of being of living beings. All of us are a blend of good and evil—the insufflated soul was marked by ambivalence, or became ambivalent by mixing itself with dust—and You died thinking about this: that Your death would eliminate the negative aspect, rid the soul of sin—all that is evil and has the capacity to do evil—leading us back to the garden or to nothingness.

The redemption that You wanted could not have had any other meaning. You knew what the chalice of salvation was, and how bitter it was to drink it, but, after the mortal uncertainty of Gethsemane, You agreed to drink it, that is, recognizing that You could not effect redemption other than by vanquishing death after having vanquished the world, You chose to die.

Many—including Your disciples—have tried to reduce Your death to human dimensions. You were killed by the reactionaries, the wealthy, the traitors of the people, the emotional plague and, above all, by the powers that be: Pontius Pilate is a Nazi governor or an imperialist general, and You a fighter for some sort of freedom, which had to be eliminated before it became a threat to the system.

In reality, nobody wanted to kill You. You were a provincial visionary, a little more exalted than the others but deprived of any political significance. All they had to do was get You out of the way and they would have been happy to let You go on living, foremost among them the procurator Pontius Pilate, now become the symbol of wickedness and repression, and instead he was the only one to behave Christianly in the long and convoluted story of Your trial.

109

But You did not want to get out of the way; You wanted to die. Everything that was written in the gospels about Your passion confirms Your obstinacy in dying, an obstinacy that had clear and distant roots, maybe not as distant as the murder of the innocents, but certainly tied to the shaping of Your precocious persuasion of being the son of God and a prophet, and therefore bound to a proximate and voluntary death. "It can't be that a prophet should die outside of Jerusalem," You had said as You set off for Jerusalem, and more than a few prophecies required precise measures of fulfillment. You wanted to die.

A lot of men want to die—the terror and the adoration of death is the terrain on which Your religion flowered—and inside each of us there is a drive to not exist, an impulse to death, which often becomes a malaise. Maybe You were affected by this malaise, but that is not enough to explain You. It was not only for delusions of grandeur—the pretense of being one God with Your father—that You wanted to die, the final proposition being to become one with all the people on earth. You died for others.

I, by betraying You, helped You die in the way You wanted, because I finally believed in Your mysterious divinity. I did what I could, and You did too; You sought Your death with sufficient dignity and steadfastness; Your majesty derided but never debased. It was not enough, and indeed we are still here, in the valley of tears. Something went wrong in the work of redemption.

What? Might one think—metaphorically—of the sleepiness, the cowardice, the unworthiness of the elect? Your becoming the Anointed, the realization of the "I am," had to be a necessity for everyone, a working together, and instead Your passion did not even have the comfort of the few that You had called and chosen. First, they fell asleep, then they ran away, leaving You alone, and the only one who would not abandon You, You had commanded to betray You.

But why then, already conscious of the abandonment, did You refuse every opportunity to save Yourself, continuing obstinately to want death? Maybe because by then, I having carried out my duty, You had to carry out Yours?

The fact is that, up to the end, You never felt alone. The agony of Gethsemane was a tormented colloquium with Your father, and You having acquiesced to do his will—what pleased him—You came to have the certainty that You would not be forsaken. Things then turned out otherwise, but meanwhile, during the whole contorted, confused, awkward trial that brought You to Your death, You felt Your father in You, and Your words never lacked the stature of the thoughts that came to You from Your father. Humanity had never been so close to salvation, or to its end.

But then nothing happened.

110

They had arrested him at Gethsemane, in the circumstances that are well known, but they didn't want to put in motion immediately a regular official proceeding. In fact, they took him to the home of Annas, a priest of great authority because he was a former high priest and he was now the father-in-law of Caiaphas, but he held no office and had no power to judge. He was an elderly and thoughtful man, much different from his son-in-law who, as far as Jesus was concerned, had already decided: it was opportune that just one man should die instead of many.

Annas interrogated Jesus, asking for information about his disciples and about his doctrine.

The Rabbi—even after his arrest he continued to behave as he had always done at the Temple, when doctors and Pharisees posed him sneaky questions: aggressive and prudent, open yet elusive—answered, "I have spoken in public, I have always taught in the synagogues and in the Temple, where all the Judeans come together, and I have never said anything in secret. Why are you interrogating me? What I have said you can ask of those who have heard me. They know what I have said."

One of the guards judged the response supercilious—after all, it seemed that Annas' right to ask questions was being contested—and he struck the Rabbi with the back of his hand.

The Rabbi took the slap but protested, submissive and dignified, "If I have spoken wrongly, show me how. But if I have spoken rightly, why must you hit me?"

Annas must have had the impression that he was a difficult prisoner; and difficult to help, assuming he even wanted to help him.

Therefore, he had him bound and sent him to Caiaphas.

111

Caiaphas was the reigning high priest and, together with other prelates, doctors of law, and eminent citizens—that is, the entire Sanhedrin united—he was waiting for the thirty dinars, which he had put in my hand a little more than three hours before, to produce some result.

Caiaphas too wanted to act quickly. Several witnesses for the prosecution were already there, convened, and they were called to depose as soon as the Rabbi arrived, but their testimony turned out not be very useful; they got confused and contradicted themselves.

Finally, two people came forward who, after affirming that they recognized Jesus of Nazareth as the bound man, declared, "This man said, 'I can destroy the Temple and rebuild it in three days.'"

It was a rather bizarre accusation, and the Rabbi could have easily deprived it of any value by proclaiming himself to be bizarre, too; many, including, and first of all, his fellow townspeople, thought that he was actually mad. In other words, it would have been to his advantage to confess that yes, he had uttered that statement, but it was an example of figurative language, the paradox being, on the level of reality, all too evident.

Instead, he said nothing, irritating even more the irritable Caiaphas, who at a certain point stood up and challenged him, "Have you got nothing to say? What can you say to these accusations advanced against you by these witnesses?"

Jesus remained silent, and remaining silent might also have been a good defense, in the sense that the accusation was so outlandish that it wasn't even the case to rebut it.

But Caiaphas's haste would not tolerate delays. Indeed, he went immediately to the heart of the matter, asking the arrestee in a sacramental formula, "I order you to tell us under oath, in the name of the living God, if you are the Anointed, the son of God."

It was a precise question, and dangerous. A wrong answer could lead directly to conviction by the Sanhedrin which, with regard to the internal justice of the Jews, was the legitimate adjudicative body.

The Rabbi thought before answering. Then he replied, "I am." And to the murmuring that greeted his concise proposition, he hurried to add words from the Book, "You shall see the son of man seated at the right hand of the All Powerful and coming with the clouds of heaven."

It was, in sum, a response that said and did not say, that lent itself to be discussed and interpreted in many ways, but Caiaphas cut off the discussion and interpreted it in the most convenient way for him. Theatrically renting his garments, he exclaimed, "He has blasphemed, what need is there of witnesses? All of you have heard his sacrilegious words. What do you think?"

It was a tribunal of power, and the defendant was one who had never concealed his aversion for their power, therefore there were no doubts or hesitations as to their reply, "He is guilty, he deserves death."

112

All well and good, he deserved death, but the Sanhedrin could not issue valid judgments in capital crimes. They were under the dominion of Rome and the prerogative of pronouncing death sentences—in their language the despots called them *jus gladii*—belonged to the Roman procurator.

This was not, habitually, a huge obstacle. Pilate was part of a nation that had a strong sense of reality and great respect for the law, but it must be conceded that such virtues, at the time of Tiberius Claudius Nero, had already quite deteriorated. The sense of reality had given way to a rational cynicism, and as concerns respect for the law, a people who had the tendency to put under their own dominion all the other peoples of the earth were not wont to put too fine a point on things. What's more, Pilate was a cultivated man from a prominent family, and he had for that people which his emperor had ordered to govern, while extracting from them a handsome sum of taxes, a coherent and genteel contempt. They were incomprehensible, litigious, obstinate, and dirty.

For all of these and other reasons, when they asked him to send one of those Jews to his death, he put no obstacles in the way. Little more than a month before, he had ordered the crucifixion of eight or nine Galileans—all much less dangerous than Jesus of Nazareth, by the way—and currently in his jails there were several felons who were waiting for him to have the good grace to put them on a cross. No doubt, therefore—so thought Caiaphas—that, asked by the Sanhedrin with which he had excellent relations, Pilate would issue a rapid and satisfying judgment.

But the sky in the east was just brightening when the Sanhedrin recognized Jesus of Nazareth as deserving of death, and a Roman procurator could not be disturbed so early in the day. Therefore, while waiting for the right hour, they left the prisoner in the custody of the guards who had arrested him, and the guards—they too possessed of a limited slice of power—amused themselves by insulting, beating, and spitting on him. Having been made aware that he proclaimed himself a prophet, they improvised a game. They covered his face with a rag, then one of them threw a punch, and they asked him, laughing, "Aren't you a prophet? Why don't you try and guess who threw the punch."

Jesus remained silent and bore it; in this too there was a prophecy to be fulfilled.

113

Then, as soon as they decently could, they conducted him, still bound, to the Roman tribunal, called the praetorium. But they did not go in; it was a profane place and the Jews—who had already purified themselves for Passover—could not enter, otherwise they would be contaminated and would not be able to eat the paschal supper.

In the end, Pilate came out to meet them, but the encounter did not go quite so smoothly as Caiaphas had hoped.

Jesus was no ordinary defendant, nor a recognized criminal, and his entrance into Jerusalem a few days before had caused too much clamor to think that he did not have some power of his own. Moreover, Pilate had a wife, and this wife of his must have seen Jesus—on the street or in the courtyards of the Temple—and certainly she had also heard tell of his facility for performing prodigies, and all things considered she had been impressed. She dreamed about him, at night, and she was superstitious. So as soon as she heard that her husband had gone outside to judge that extraordinary Jesus of Nazareth, she sent to tell him, "Avoid any relationship with that individual because, in my dreams, he upset me."

Pilate had a cultural background and moral stature that was surely superior to his wife's. Nevertheless, her warning accentuated his attention for the prisoner. He was young and, although badly beaten—there were numerous signs of blows to his face—he emanated charm and mystery. Pilate asked the Jews, "Of what do you accuse this man?"

Relations between the Jewish Sanhedrin and the Roman procurator were excellent, but very prudent, contorted, captious; the Jews especially didn't like taking compromising positions. So, they responded in a noncommittal way, "If he weren't a miscreant we wouldn't have brought him to you."

They still hadn't understood that Pilate had an attitude toward this prisoner that was different from how he might have felt on previous occasions about other moribund defendants. Indeed, he said, "Take him and judge him yourselves according to your laws."

The response of the Jews was quite clever, "We cannot pronounce a death sentence."

They wanted to signify their complete recognition of the domination of Rome and even more their conviction that for this prisoner there was no possible sentence other than the death penalty.

And the Roman procurator had the right—and even the duty—to pronounce the *jus gladii*. In sum, a formality.

114

But Pilate wanted to see his way clear.

He went back into the praetorium, had the prisoner brought in, and interrogated him without the Jews in the way. He must have already been well informed about the bizarre behavior of that Jesus, and he asked him a surprise question, "Are you the king of the Jews?"

It was a political question, and up to now politics had remained on the margins of the affair.

The Rabbi asked in turn, "Is this your question or was it suggested to you by others?"

This was a match, in conditions of obvious imparity, between two men from two different worlds, but both with a high intelligence quotient. One was a high-level Roman functionary, the other an ordinary Galilean who nevertheless, when he had to define himself, used the proposition, "I am." And now he was insinuating—perhaps—that the Roman procurator was relying on questions suggested by Caiaphas.

Pilate replied, "Am I perhaps a Jew? Your people and your priests have delivered you to me. What have you done?"

The question was generic but, vaguely, it included the previous one; did he perhaps believe himself to be the king of the Jews?

The prisoner's response was high-sounding, noble, and splendidly evasive, "My kingdom is not of this world. If my kingdom were of this world, my followers would have fought to make sure I did not fall into the hands of the Jews. But my kingdom is not here."

Maybe he was a little too ingenuous, or generous, to think that his followers would have fought for him—those eleven that he had kept, anyway—but his answer was on the mark and tended to shift the issue onto a terrain that was irrelevant for Roman law, and certainly Pilate had no desire to concern himself with heavenly kingdoms. But the response was also, as often was the case, ambiguous. His kingdom may not have been here, but it could not be excluded that it was in another city or region, perhaps in some way connected to Rome.

Pilate wanted concrete answers, not word games. So he asked directly, "So, are you or are you not king?"

Jesus of Nazareth had schooled himself, aristocratically, on the scriptures of the Eternal, therefore he felt himself much superior to one who believed in false and mendacious gods and idols. To the question, which sounded disrespectful and arrogant, he responded, "You say it: I am king. For this I was born, and I came into the world: to testify to the truth. Whoever is for the truth listens to my voice."

Pilate had schooled himself, much more modestly, on Latin and Greek authors of the decadence, therefore he asked, "What is the truth?" and he didn't even wait for the answer because, to his way of thinking, there could be no answer.

115

Rabbi, Jesus, Yeshua in our sweet language.

That man, Pilate, he too on the way to becoming an enduring symbol of evil, was pulled out of the darkness of the centuries and of human history, and for four hours he entered into Your life so that the imaginary would have a confrontation with the real. Without You, nobody would remember him, but without him maybe You would also be forgotten: Bethlehem, Nazareth, Capernaum, Bethany, Your probable death by stoning, Your teaching and Your prodigies, Your encounters with the angels and the demons, would have rapidly become passages of a nebulous and uncertain legend difficult to recall, wouldn't have had confirmation in the history that later, for lack of anything better, permitted the spread of Your thought throughout the world.

Rome: force, power, dominion, reality.

Yet it was precisely that Roman idolater, apparently so rooted in visible things, who posed You in the highest form and the most appropriate manner—what is the truth?—that question without an answer that others asked You in such an earthly manner: Who is Your father? Where is Your father? Show us Your father.

"Father," You had prayed a short time before, at the end of the last supper, "sanctify them in the truth: Your word is the truth."

You could not respond to that procurator who was looking for concrete things—are you or are you not king?—"the truth is the word of my father with whom I am one, in the expectation that everyone will be one in us."

An answer so formulated, in any event, wouldn't have satisfied even us, inclined to infinite spiritual complications with a single, unnamable, and invisible God, and nevertheless tormented by uncertainty, questions, the anxiety to know, understand, see, touch.

You gave no answer, and we still suffer the deficit. You, perhaps, thought You would give the answer a little while later, with the glory, but that not having happened, we continue to ask ourselves, what is truth.

Paul later wrote that faith is the certainty of hoped-for things, the demonstration of invisible things. A satisfaction that is inscrutably given, a crossing over into the eternal spheres.

Rabbi, for us—those to whom not enough of it is given— faith might consist in not asking questions, not of the Eternal, nor of You, nor of ourselves.

But this too crosses over into the eternal spheres of non-life, and maybe the only way is not to expect answers to questions that cannot have any.

And Pilate was not irritated by Your silence. He felt for You—above and beyond his wife's suggestion—that vague admiration that those who believe in nothing have for those who believe in something; he didn't want to send You to Golgotha.

He was reminded that You were a Galilean, and therefore from the jurisdiction of Herod, and since Herod was in

Jerusalem for Passover, he thought it best to send You to him, so that it would be him to put You to death, if there was absolutely no way to avoid it.

And, so, You confronted the most grotesque part of Your ridiculous trial.

116

Herod was a peculiar king. He had John the Baptist's head cut off, but, in essence, without wishing him ill, in obeisance to his wicked wife, and, to tell it as it is, thanks in part to a young lass who was a rather audacious dancer. For Jesus of Nazareth, he had a great, and dangerous, curiosity. He had heard a lot of talk about that subject of his who performed extraordinary prodigies with extraordinary facility, and he couldn't wait to have him before him. Maybe he could even get him to perform some strictly personal prodigy for himself.

Therefore, when they brought him to the palace, he was overjoyed, but then quickly disappointed; it appeared that Jesus of Nazareth had no desire whatsoever, at the moment, to perform miracles. Despite finding himself in a rather precarious, not to say completely compromised, position, he did not appreciate being treated like a magician or a juggler. So, he shut himself up in his pride, which was not lacking.

Herod interrogated him at length, asking him all kinds of questions, mostly quite odd. Jesus remained silent the whole time. Herod could easily have had his head cut off too, with no problem at all.

But, and if he was the Baptist restored to life, as some were saying? And if he was even greater than the Baptist, as many were saying?

While he mulled, things were taking a turn for the worse. The high priests and doctors of law were there—they could go to him with no fear of being contaminated—and they were menacingly demanding judgment.

Herod didn't feel up to it and he rushed to send the prisoner back to Pilate. Herod was in the city for private reasons, for worship, and besides, the Galilean, though he was by reason of his origins under his jurisdiction, had allegedly committed the crimes he was accused of in Jerusalem, so let the procurator handle it.

With Jesus, however, Herod was more than a little annoyed, for his stubborn silence and his refusal to perform prodigies, and so, to scorn him and mock him, he had him wear a splendid mantle—wasn't he charged with claiming to be king?—and so costumed he gave him back to the Roman soldiers to be taken back to him who had sent him.

117

When they informed him that Herod had sent back the prisoner, the Roman procurator again had to leave the praetorium and again deal with that fastidious problem, again get involved in discussions with the high priests, community leaders, the whole populace of that odious city.

But as to the sentence they were asking him for, he didn't want to concede. He said, "You have brought this man to appear before me, accusing him of inciting the people to revolt, but I have not found him guilty of any of the crimes of which you accuse him. And neither has Herod, to the point that he has sent him back to me. In brief, this man has not committed any crime punishable by death."

The high priests, community leaders, and the people—the same people who only days before had shouted themselves hoarse with hosannas—demonstrated their discontent by shaking their fists and creating a ruckus.

Pilate was not a man to give in to threats from an odoriferous gaggle of Jews; their stench, revivified by their agitation, was wafting up from the square below. However, he needed to find some legal way of resisting them, and it was not easy. Finally, an idea came to him.

It was customary, among the Jews, to pardon a prisoner during the occasion of the Passover, one who would delight the crowd. Now, in prison, he had an extremist by the name of Barabbas, who had been jailed because, at the head of a gang of dissidents, he had provoked disorders and committed murder.

The extremists were not loved by anyone, not even by the zealots, because, with their excesses, they did the cause more harm than good. What's more, the merchants detested them since, anytime they succeeded in putting together a fair or some promotional activity, the extremists took advantage of the occasion to overturn stands, loot shops, sack the houses of the wealthy, set random fires, and so on. The priests and Pharisees hated them because they were utterly bereft of religious sentiment; their aspiration was to destroy all forms of power, even if it derived from the Eternal, and violence was their means of self-realization.

Pilate sent his soldiers, therefore, to get Barabbas out of jail, sure that the crowd, and the priests too, would ask for the liberation of the Galilean who, at least, was not violent. He was wrong; he didn't take into account either Caiaphas's personal dislike for Jesus or the point of view of the zealots for whom, at that point, it was important that it be the Romans to put to death that young fanatic who, after his death, would be easily exalted as a true prophet. And the zealots, that day, were quite numerous in the crowd, had come out in force, given the opportunity, in the square in front of the praetorium.

So, when Pilate presented Jesus and Barabbas at the same time, and asked—so sure of himself as to permit himself a little humor—if they wanted him to liberate the king of the Jews, they surprisingly answered no, that they didn't want him freed, on the contrary they shouted at the top of their voices: "Crucify him! Crucify him!"

Pilate was not delighted by opposition, at least not when it came from a crowd of Jews. He raised a hand to ask for a semblance of quiet, and said with all the voice he could muster, "But what wrong has he done to you? I have not found in him any crime punishable by death. I will give him back his freedom."

The crowd didn't want to hear it. They had been incited by the zealots and the priests, but now they were also beginning to draw energy from their own force, to have the pleasing temptation to use it against the will of the procurator of Caesar. Their cries of "Crucify him and give us Barabbas!" were growing louder and more unified.

"What wrong has he done to you?" Pilate shouted again, but the tumult only grew louder.

Then he had a basin of water brought out and he washed his hands in front of the crowd, saying, "I am innocent of the death of this just man. This is your affair."

"Let his blood fall on us and on our children!" the crowd shouted, recklessly.

118

Pilate was forced to free Barabbas, a man who had been imprisoned for insurrection and homicide. Such was the choice of the crowd, and to that choice he was obliged.

But on Jesus he did not want to give in. He was standing there, the Galilean, his head down, resigned to his fate, and Herod's mantle was no longer on his shoulders. It was a splendid mantle, and they had stolen it from him.

Strange man, the prisoner; he had more will to die than to live, it seemed. There was something irreducible in him, a force that surely came from his God, and Caiaphas was anxious that he be crucified because he feared him; he was too rabid in wanting his death.

But he, Pilate, had nothing to fear, on the contrary, he would have been quite content if a popular movement, born in the provinces, should overthrow the clique that lorded over Jerusalem: contorted, treacherous, clever Jews. Therefore, he made a final attempt to save him. It made him angry that he should have to use his irreducible strength to remain passive under the hostility of the crowd. What would he get out of death, a death so terribly ferocious?

He had him brought back inside the praetorium and ordered his soldiers to flagellate him.

Flagellation was a cruel punishment, which often provoked the death of the victim, so it could be considered a substitute for the death penalty. The Roman soldiers possessed a portion of power undoubtedly superior to that of the guards of the Sanhedrin, and accordingly their ferocity was more robust, their meanness more refined. Indeed, they were not satisfied just to flagellate him vigorously, so they also made a crown of thorns and placed it on his head—like a king—and they covered his shoulders with a purple mantle—like a king—and they slapped his face, saying, "Hail, king of the Jews!"

This, for the soldiers, might also be an amusement, the more so because it allowed for a pinch of racism and a bit of resentment for having to serve so far from home, in a foreign country where they were not loved. Pilate let them do as they wished. Maybe, rather than giving the Jews the satisfaction of crucifying him on Golgotha, he preferred that the young man should die there, in the praetorium, from the beating. But more than likely he had the intention of presenting to the tumultuous crowd gathered outside a poor wretch reduced to such a pitiful state that it would be impossible not to pity him.

He went out protected by a goodly number of soldiers and confronted the Jews again, "Now I show him to you so that you will know that I find no guilt in him."

119

Held up by the same soldiers who had flagellated him, Jesus was led outside; bleeding, debilitated by the beating, dispirited from the insults, ridiculously dressed as a king, with a purple mantle and a crown of thorns. And Pilate shouted, "Behold the man!"

He expected an outpouring of pity for him.

But the priests and the guards of the Sanhedrin and the zealots erupted in a chorus of shouting, "Crucify him! Crucify him!" and the people took up the cry in turn, in a menacing crescendo.

Pilate kept Jesus firmly in the hands of his soldiers, but the crowd was frightening. He shouted, "You take him to crucify him because I have found no basis for charging him."

For the priests this proposal could have been acceptable—for them it was enough that the Galilean be eliminated—but not for the zealots. They wanted it to be the Romans who killed him. So, the Jews responded to Pilate's proposal with an ambiguous response, "We have a law, and according to the law he must die because he claims to be the son of God."

They were back to where it all started: for the Roman law the accusation was groundless or at the very least insignificant, but according to the law of occupation, it was up to the

Roman procurator to validate the death sentence issued in accordance with Jewish law.

Pilate could feel his anger rising. Apart from everything else, it was almost noon, and his whole morning had been taken up with this annoying affair of this man who wanted to be the son of God. What did it matter to him? Didn't these miserable Jews have some other quibble to bother about?

But he continued to feel compassion and sympathy for the young Galilean; it upset him that he should die. He thought that at this point it wouldn't be that hard for him to get himself out of it, all he had to do was declare, somehow or other, that he was not claiming to be the son of God.

Pilate managed to get him back inside the praetorium, away from the clamor and pressure of the crowd. He asked him, to begin with, "Where are you from?"

Strange. It wasn't a realistic question; everyone knew that the prisoner was from Nazareth in Galilee. But it could also have been realistic, in the sense that Pilate wanted to know if he wanted to insist on this madness of proclaiming himself the son of God.

But it appeared that he did not want to answer.

And Pilate started getting irritated with him too, "Do you refuse to answer me? Don't you know that I have the power to release you or crucify you?"

The way things stood maybe even Pilate did not have as much power as he claimed. In any case, the Rabbi decided to answer him, "You would have no power over me if it had not been given you from on high. Therefore, the responsibility of those who have given me into your hands is greater."

He had the habit of expressing himself with words that were high-sounding and obscure. Did from on high, for him, mean from that God of the Jews who couldn't even be called by name, or from Caesar, who in a way was also a god himself? The procurator was free to choose; if the question was of any interest to him. Anyway, the prisoner was absolving him of any grave responsibility; the priests had more responsibility, and on this at least he felt himself in agreement.

Despite himself, Pilate continued to be bound by his intelligence, by his capacity for forbearance, by the inexplicable majesty of that young man who had more will to die than to live, and yet again, he tried to snatch him away from death.

He went out and informed the crowd that he intended to release him.

The priests and zealots had had time to further instruct the people. The Jews shouted in unison, "If you release him, you are not a friend of Caesar; he who proclaims himself king defies Caesar."

The insinuation was ridiculous; it took a lot more than a remnant of purple cloth and a crown of thorns to defy Caesar. But the Jews were devious, capable of sending a delegation to Rome to tell tales of stuff and nonsense, and Tiberius, for his part, was even more devious than the Jews. Suddenly, the procurator found himself in a dangerous situation.

But he didn't want to give up the fight. After all, it was past noon, all he had to do was drag it out a little longer and then there wouldn't be time for a crucifixion because of the feast day.

He ordered his soldiers to take Jesus back outside, making him take a place on a rostrum that was used for official communications. He let the people get a good idea of the condition the prisoner was in; more dead than alive, bleeding and beaten, ridiculous in the purple mantle and the crown of thorns.

The procurator pointed at him and said to the crowd of Jews, "Behold, your king!"

As though to say, who could submit that someone reduced to that state could be a danger to Caesar?

But the crowd, by now incapable of pity, cried out again for crucifixion.

Pilate—it was his last pathetic attempt—shouted, "Must I crucify your king?"

From the crowd the priests responded, "We have no king other than Caesar."

So, the procurator—even his wife would understand that more than this could not be done—released him to them; let them to do as they wished.

120

I had followed You, Jesus, since my betrayal, through all the passages of Your passion, of Your torment.

Now I'm following You toward Golgotha. It's too dark to see, despite its being just past noon, the sky has clouded over, and darkness has fallen on the earth. The Eternal, moved to pity at last, is finally giving signs. The air is still, heavy, and lightning bolts of a brightness never seen are shooting up from the horizon and splitting the sky, and it's not a storm but the power of God. Ancient scriptures are coming true, in an unforeseen manner, however, without much splendor.

Pilate has provided an escort of soldiers, not more than a dozen, but commanded by an officer. Justice is Roman. A few Jews, drawn from the lower classes, are gathered around You, destined to be the material executors of the crucifixion, if there will be a crucifixion. The prophecies are tenuous, and this involves the son of God, innumerable possibilities stand before his power.

They have forced a Cyrenian to carry Your cross; You had no more strength. There are no disciples to be seen. A handful of women is following You at a distance. They have been with us since Galilee. They took care of You, now they are desperate. They don't know that the sky is full of angels that are about to rip it open with light. The power of the Eternal will be fully manifested, but we are still climbing toward the gloom and the pain, and the pious women come to a halt, exhausted.

But You are not alone, Jesus; Your father who sent You is with You, he does not leave You, does not forsake You. In some way You are doing his will, what inexplicably pleases him. You are drinking the cup of salvation. You are carrying all the sins of the world. You are immolating Yourself for Your sheep. You are leading humanity back to the Garden of Eden or to the infinite time of God, wherever there is no desperation, no knowledge of good and evil, no horror of death. The world You have already vanquished; now You will vanquish life, so that all will be one with You and with Your father.

All but me, perhaps. I will not have Your glory, but an ordinary peace, after a death of expiation. I know that by now it is near, the mark around my neck has become evident, like that of the Baptist shortly before he was taken. Will there still be a resurrection on the last day?

I was in the courtyard of Caiaphas when the Sanhedrin were judging You deserving of death, and then I saw the guards who insulted You and beat You. I did not do or say anything. I was at Herod's when his guards scorned and offended You. I did not intervene, I was in front of the praetorium when Pilate proposed Jesus or Barabbas, and I did not shout Barabbas, but neither did I shout Jesus. That which had been established I had carried out; now it was Your turn.

I suffered for You as You had suffered for me when You condemned me to betray You, but the will from on high had to be done. With anguish You were going toward death, but Your steadfastness in suffering was bitter and magnificent; I mustn't obstruct the path that You had chosen. I saw You, in desperation, worn out, pallid, bloody, I forced myself to think You didn't feel any pain—how can the son of God feel pain, one who can command legions of angels—but Your pain was so evident that it had to be real.

Perhaps the pain was necessary for You to become the son of God. Your becoming had not yet reached its end.

121

Now the end is drawing near, interminable journey, as You climb to the place of the skull. The heavens and the earth are preparing for the event: darkness, lightning, rumbling blasts that are not thunder, but an earthquake on its way. It will be the end of time, let it mean whatever it wants to mean.

Will You save me too, Rabbi? Save me if You can. I know I still have some evil in me—it entered me when You gave me the dipped morsel—but if You want, it will abandon me. Not my will, however, but Yours be done.

Golgotha is near. You struggle to drag Yourself along behind the Cyrenian who carries Your cross, shut inside Your struggle, trusting that You are not alone: You have Your father, You know You have him, and so even Your anguish is beautiful, Your suffering comfort. The greater the pain, the closer the glory. Blessed are they. But, Jesus, don't make me suffer more than what is just. I have done my part, and my desperation is sterile; it does not produce salvation.

We have reached Golgotha and it appears You will be crucified. The Cyrenian has put down Your cross. You will have to drink Your chalice all the way to the end. Bitter is the salvation of man. But Your father wills it, and he does not forsake You.

There, You are crucified, nailed to the cross still on the ground. They are about to hoist You up between two other crosses on which have been hung two criminals. For this, too, there are scriptures to be fulfilled. Pagan soldiers draw lots for Your clothes; more scriptures. Whoever feels like it, mocks You, even the two criminals on either side of You; they are still men.

Your face, where there is no stain of blood—a woman managed to wipe it clean as best she could during the climb—is pallid as it was under the crown of thorns. You keep Your eyes closed, but You are still breathing. Death is long to vanquish; has the Eternal no pity?

The sky grows ever darker, the booming ever bleaker, the lightning more frequent, the earthquake shakes the mountain, every part of creation leans toward the place of the skull where the Anointed, the son of God, is vanquishing death.

There, You open Your eyes again, in the lightning flashes You make out some Roman soldiers, some sordid, sniggering Jews. Is this the part of humanity that has followed You to make Your becoming possible? Beyond the pain, is there no one to soothe the heartbreak?

The darkness destroys me, the gloom covers my face.

The chalice is finished, You are about to die. Where is Your father? David's lament issues from Your mouth, "My God, my God, why have you forsaken me?"

There is no answer.

Then, with a cry, You render up Your spirit.

The earth quakes more powerfully, the veil of the Temple is rent in two, I run to my final desperation.

O Eternal, I cry out to you from places far too deep. Lord, do not heed my voice.

Notes on Contributors

GIUSEPPE BERTO (1914–1978) started writing novels when he was a prisoner of war in Hereford, Texas, from 1943 to 1946. The second novel he wrote there, *Il cielo è rosso* (1947), was the first to be published, and it was a commercial and critical success, winning praise from Ernest Hemingway and the Florence Prize for literature. This first success was followed quickly by two others, *Le opere di Dio* (1948) and *Il brigante* (1951). Both *Il cielo è rosso* and *Il brigante* were later made into films.

His first three novels earned Berto a prominent place among Italy's renowned generation of postwar writers. He never felt at home in the literary establishment, however, and was not embraced by it, partly because of his fascist past, and partly because of his discomfort with any form of authority. As a young man, Berto had been a convinced fascist, joining the avanguardisti in 1929 and volunteering to fight in Ethiopia in 1935 and again in North Africa in 1941. More importantly for his postwar relationship with his literary peers, Berto never recanted his youthful adherence to fascism.

Underlying Berto's sense of alienation and perhaps also his attraction to fascism was his difficult relationship with authority, starting with his own father. His struggle with authority was a root cause of a serious neurosis that kept Berto from writing during the 1950s, and it was the central theme of his masterpiece that ended his long silence, *Il male oscuro*, which won both the Campiello Prize and the Viareggio Prize in 1964 and was made into a film by Mario Monicelli.

In several of his works, including his first two novels and his last novel *La gloria* (1978), Berto elaborated his existential struggle in confrontations with Christianity.

GREGORY CONTI was born and raised in Pittsburgh and has a BA from Notre Dame, an MA from Yale, and a JD from Yale Law School. He practiced law as a legal services lawyer in New Haven, Connecticut, and Waltham, Massachussetts, for five years before moving to Perugia in 1985. Since then he has taught English at the University of Perugia and the Foreign Language School of the Italian Army, and Italian History at the University of Rochester (Arezzo). In the fall of 2013 he was visiting professor in the Department of Italian at Rutgers University. Since his first published book translation in 1998, he has published some thirty volumes of fiction, nonfiction, and poetry with university presses and publishers in the United States. In addition to Giuseppe Berto, the authors he has translated include Emilio Lussu, Rosetta Loy, Elisa Biagini, Sebastiano Vassalli, Paolo Rumiz, Stefano Mancuso, Alberto Angela, Igiaba Scego, and Edoardo Nesi.

ALESSANDRO VETTORI is professor of Italian and comparative literature at Rutgers University–New Brunswick, where he serves as chair of the Department of Italian. He has written monographs and edited books on Dante, Boccaccio, Francis of Assisi, Iacopone da Todi, and Giuseppe Berto. He is the editor of *Italian Quarterly*, and he coedits the translation series Other Voices of Italy with Rutgers University Press.